WITCHBLADE®

REDEMPTION VOLUME 1

written by:
Ron Marz

art by:
Stjepan Sejic

Witchblade created by:
Marc Silvestri, David Wohl,
Brian Haberlin and Michael Turner

published by
Top Cow Productions, Inc.
Los Angeles

WITCHBLADE

REDEMPTION VOLUME 1

written by: **Ron Marz**
art by: **Stjepan Sejic**
letters by: **Troy Peteri**

•••••

For this edition cover art by: **Stjepan Sejic**
Original editions edited by: **Filip Sablik & Phil Smith**
For this edition book design and layout by: **Phil Smith**
Witchblade logo design by: **Todd Klein**

for Top Cow Productions Inc.
Marc Silvestri - Chief Executive Officer • **Matt Hawkins** - President and Chief Operating Officer
Filip Sablik - Publisher • **Phil Smith** - Managing Editor • **Atom Freeman** - Director of Sales and Marketing
Bryan Rountree - Assistant to Publisher • **Christine Dinh** - Marketing Assistant
Mark Haynes - Webmaster • **Ernest Gomez, Anthony McAfee** - Interns

for *image* comics
publisher:
Eric Stephenson

Witchblade: Redemption volume 1 Trade Paperback November 2010. FIRST PRINTING.
BOOK MARKET EDITION ISBN: 978-1-60706-193-9, $9.99 U.S.D..
Published by Image Comics Inc. Office of Publication: 2134 Allston Way, 2nd Floor Berkeley, CA 94704. Originally published in single magazine form as WITCHBLADE 131-136. **PRINTED IN KOREA.**

Table of Contents

Introduction

As someone who's been in the comic book industry for well over two decades, the one piece of our industry's history that's been prevalent is that males have dominated it. Whether it be from an artistic point of view, or on the writing or editorial side, males have filled a majority of the comic book industry roles. Additionally, if most people make a list of the top superhero characters from American comic book lore, the ones that jump out readily are male figures. Female characters in this landscape, for the most part, have rarely been given the chance to be equal with their male counterparts. However, there have been a few throughout history. Most of us would put Wonder Woman on a list of the top ten or twenty. Sadly, once you get past her name, most people start to stutter, and don't have too many obvious choices. Perhaps Sue Storm comes to mind from the *Fantastic Four*, or a couple of the female leads from *X-Men.* My point is there's a moment of hesitation as you try to gather your thoughts of top female characters. However, one character undeniably earned her right to be included in this list, and that's *Witchblade.*

Years ago, Marc Silvestri, along with the late Michael Turner, created a book knowing the odds, arguably, were already stacked against them with a lead female character. Unlike my character, *Spawn*, who fell into the standard formula of male superhero comics, they decided to stretch their creative talents a little bit further and pushed the odds. You're now holding issues number 131-136, and this book is fast approaching its 200th issue. That lone statistic may put *Witchblade* at the number two spot for the longest running, top selling female comic. Very few other female driven titles are able to tout an issue count over 100, let alone 200! That statistic is where the power of this book is!

Once you have a female as the lead character, you pepper it with some obvious trappings. Normally, a female character is nice to look at. They're lovely, curvy, and in good shape. As artists, we usually try to make them a little more scantily clad—it's a just a byproduct of men being able to come up with the design for women's costumes. We like to make them very impractical so we can either see a lot of skin, or at least the curve and silhouette of the female form. We still want to see that hourglass figure. However, you still have to get past that impractical part and lay a great foundation and back-story for the character.

As someone who's been intrigued by characters like Batman, my creative bent has always been dark and moody images and storylines, and Witchblade falls right into that sweet spot. She came out of the gate as a bit of a mystery, but has been able to build her back-story for well over a decade, and has worked successfully, not only in the comic book industry, but also television, toys, and now a potential film. She's become a pop culture icon, which is about as successful as you can get for any character.

After all these years, Marc Silvestri, has been able to take his creative force, fuse it with a great start that was given to him by Top Cow, Image Comics, and Mike Turner, and pushed this character forward so that I'm now able to be sitting here writing a foreword for a trade paperback that's approaching it's 15th or 16th year of existence. That in and of itself is the biggest congratulatory statement I can extend. Anyone who starts any comic book, any creative process, and ten, fifteen, or twenty years down the road can say they're still producing that same comic book is on a very hard path to go down at any point of any career in any industry. And although one of the great creative inspirations behind this character is no longer with us, his creative child is still alive and well. To have a character or brand name that is still viable proves Marc and Michael hit a homerun from what they set out to do. I hope there will be an unending number of issues released of *Witchblade*, and that fifteen years from now, I'll be writing another foreword stating how fantastic this property is.

Todd McFarlane

September 2010, Phoenix, Arizona

From budding baseball player to comic book artist extraordinaire to family man, Spawn creator Todd McFarlane has a wealth of experience in the world of entertainment. Today, McFarlane, his wife, Wanda, and their three children reside in Arizona, where Todd maintains a happily hectic balance between his family and all his interests (sports, film, comics, action figures).

Thus far in...

WITCHBLADE

Sara Pezzini's life was already complicated with her job as a New York City Police Detective.

But then she came into possession of an ancient and powerful artifact known as the Witchblade, forcing Sara to balance her police career and the supernatural weapon.

Eventually, Sara learned the Witchblade was actually meant to serve as the balance between the two primal forces in the universe, the Darkness and the Angelus.

When Sara discovered she was pregnant with a child fathered by Darkness host Jackie Estacado, she decided to pass the Witchblade on to another bearer.

The Witchblade ended up in the hands of Danielle Baptiste, an aspiring dancer who was also the daughter of Sara's police captain.

Following the birth of her daughter, Hope, Sara reclaimed half of the Witchblade, while Dani retained the other half.

Unknown to either of them at the time, the Witchblade had split along its Darkness and Angelus components.

Sara possessed the dark half of the Witchblade, and Dani the light half. The malign nature of the Darkness influenced Sara's behavior.

Inevitably, Sara and Dani clashed in a brutal confrontation. In the aftermath, Sara was herself again, and in possession of the rejoined Witchblade, but Dani was mortally wounded.

Dani's life was saved by the embodiment of the Angelus power, which selected her to serve as its new host.

Sara was left with the memories of what she'd done, knowing she would have to make amends.

Now she tries to rebuild a life that includes her police partner and lover, Detective Patrick Gleason, and her sister, Julie.

"Just Like Starting Over"

DON'T MAKE ME *ANGRY.*
YOU WOULDN'T *LIKE ME* WHEN I'M ANGRY.
NOT *BUYING* IT, ARE YOU?
BYOOP!
COME ON, HOPE, GIVE AUNTIE JULES A BREAK HERE. CAN WE AT LEAST *TRY* TO GET MORE FOOD IN YOUR MOUTH THAN ON THE CEILING?
WORLD'S BEST MOMMY
NY
I BROUGHT *GROCERIES,* PEZZINI!
PREPARE TO REWARD ME WITH *SEXUAL FAVORS!*
WELL, OKAY, GLEASON...

...BUT MY *SISTER* MIGHT BE A LITTLE MIFFED IF SHE COMES HOME TO FIND US DOING IT ON THE KITCHEN TABLE.

OOPS.

AND YOU KNOW HOW SHE IS WHEN *SHE* GETS ANGRY.

SORRY, JULIE. NOT QUITE USED TO YOU CRASHING HERE.

SARA'S NOT AROUND?

RIGHT ON THE FIRST TRY. YOU SHOULD BE A *DETECTIVE.*

SHE WENT OUT FOR A *JOG.* I'M SURPRISED SHE'S NOT BACK YET.

SHE'S PROBABLY STAYING AWAY UNTIL THE FEEDING FRENZY IS DONE.
YOU'RE WELCOME TO TAKE OVER ANY TIME YOU WANT, BY THE WAY.

YEAH, THANKS BUT NO. I'VE BEEN DOWN THAT ROAD AND HAD THE MASHED BANANAS IN MY HAIR TO PROVE IT.
HOPE INHERITED HER MAMA'S STUBBORN STREAK, SO SHE'S ALL YOURS.

YOU KNOW, THIS IS GOOD, ACTUALLY. YOU AND I HAVEN'T HAD MUCH OF A CHANCE TO TALK SINCE I MOVED IN.

ABOUT...?
YOU KNOW... EVERYTHING.
SARA AND I WEREN'T EXACTLY PEN PALS WHEN I WAS IN PRISON. THERE'S A LOT WE STILL HAVEN'T CAUGHT UP ON...

"...AND I WANT TO FIND OUT WHAT'S GOING ON IN MY SISTER'S LIFE."
DROP IT, ASSHOLE!
"THE COP PART? OR THE WITCHBLADE PART?"
"BOTH, I GUESS. ALL OF IT."

DON'T HURT THE KID!
I'M A **COP!** DON'T HURT THE KID AND WE CAN **ALL** WALK AWAY FROM THIS.
KEEP BACK!
"WELL, **SOME** OF IT YOU ALREADY KNOW, RIGHT?

BULLSHIT!
YOU AIN'T NO **COP,** NOT DRESSED LIKE **THAT!**
"SHE ENDED UP WITH A LETTER OF REPRIMAND IN HER JACKET OVER NOT REPORTING TO WORK WHEN EVERYTHING WAS GOING ON WITH DANI.

"OTHER THAN THAT, NO REAL **FALLOUT.** LET'S BE HONEST, SHE'S A DAMN GOOD COP.
COPS GO JOGGING TOO.
NOW JUST LET THE KID **GO** AND WE'LL FIGURE THIS OUT. WHATEVER SHE WALKED INTO HERE, DRUG DEAL GONE BAD OR WHATEVER, SHE'S NOT PART OF--

BACK OFF, BITCH! NOT ANOTHER **STEP!**
BLAM
"WHEN YOU'RE **THAT** GOOD, THE DEPARTMENT FINDS A WAY TO KEEP YOU ON THE JOB."

"WHAT ABOUT YOUR CAPTAIN? SHE'S DANI'S MOTHER, RIGHT? SHE HAS TO HAVE FIGURED OUT... SOMETHING.
DON'T MAKE ME DRAG YOU, BRAT!
YOU HURT THAT KID...
...I'M THE WORST GOD DAMN ENEMY YOU EVER HAD.
"SHE MUST AT LEAST KNOW SARA HAS SOME UNUSUAL TASTE IN JEWELRY."
"CAPTAIN PEYROUX REALIZES SOMETHING IS UP. HOW COULD SHE NOT?
GET IN HERE!
"BUT SO FAR SHE'S IGNORED IT, JUST LIKE SHE'S IGNORED OUR RELATIONSHIP. DON'T ASK, DON'T TELL.
"WORKING IN THE SPECIAL CASES DIVISION ISN'T THE EASIEST DUTY IN THE P.D.
SHIT...
...AIN'T NO WAY OUT.
"PEYROUX'S WILLING TO LOOK THE OTHER WAY AS LONG AS WE'RE GETTING THE JOB DONE."

"WHAT ABOUT THE REST? THE WITCHBLADE PART?
DON'T EVEN TWITCH.
DROP THE GUN AND TURN AROUND SLOWLY.
VERY SLOWLY.
"SHE'S GOT ALL OF IT AGAIN, WHICH IS GOOD, RIGHT? SHE'S COMPLETELY OVER WHAT HAPPENED TO HER WHEN IT WAS SPLIT?"
I'M WALKING OUT OF HERE, AND YOU AIN'T GONNA DO SHIT TO STOP ME.
NOT UNLESS YOU WANT THIS BRAT'S BRAINS ON YOUR CONSCIENCE AND ON THE FLOOR.
PLEASE, THAT HURTS...
"YOU TELL ME. YOU'RE THE ONE WHO'S BEEN LIVING HERE WITH HER.
"SARA GOT PULLED PRETTY FAR OVER TO THE DARK SIDE. SHE SEEMS LIKE HERSELF...
"...BUT WHO KNOWS WHAT THAT DOES TO A PERSON?"
WHAT THE HELL IS THAT THING?
FROM THE LOOK OF IT...
...HUNGRY.
"SHE'S A LITTLE DISTANT, BUT I THOUGHT IT WAS BECAUSE THERE'S STILL SO MUCH THAT'S UNRESOLVED BETWEEN US. TELL ME SOMETHING...

"...DO YOU TRUST HER?"
I USED TO BE ABLE TO CONTROL THIS THING. THESE DAYS...
...I'M NOT SO SURE.
I GOT THE GUN, I'M IN CHARGE HERE! YOU KEEP THAT AWAY FROM ME!
"I TRUST HER...
YOU'RE IN A DEAD END. HAND OVER THE GUN AND LET THE GIRL GO.
KEEP YOUR DISTANCE! YOU'RE SOME KINDA FREAK!
"...BUT NOW I'VE SEEN THAT OTHER SIDE OF HER, WHEN THE DARKNESS TOOK OVER.
YOU'LL BE OKAY, SWEETIE. I'M NOT GOING TO LET ANYTHING HAPPEN TO YOU.
"I DON'T MIND ADMITTING IT WAS SCARY.
GET BACK!
PLEASE...
"AND THAT TICKLES AT THE BACK OF MY MIND, WONDERING IF WHAT WAS UNLEASHED THEN IS STILL IN THERE SOMEWHERE. WAITING.

"SO YEAH, I DO TRUST SARA...
"...BUT NOT THAT DAMN THING ON HER WRIST.
"IT NEVER BOTHERED ME WHEN I WAS SURE SHE WAS THE ONE CALLING THE SHOTS, NOT THE WITCHBLADE. NOW...
"...HARD TO KNOW, ISN'T IT?
YAAGH!
"I FIND MYSELF WONDERING 'IS THAT ALL SARA?' OR, IS THERE SOMETHING ELSE TRYING TO GET OUT?
STOP IT...
GHHH...
"AND IF THERE IS, CAN SHE PULL IT BACK?"
...STOP...

"GREAT, NOW YOU'LL HAVE ME SLEEPING WITH ONE EYE OPEN."
"NO, DON'T TAKE WHAT I'M SAYING THE WRONG WAY. SARA IS THE SAME SARA.
"BUT I THINK I SEE THE WITCHBLADE A LITTLE DIFFERENTLY THAN I DID BEFORE.
HNNNGH...
"AND MAYBE THAT'S NOT SUCH A BAD THING."
"CAN'T BE EASY TO HAVE THAT KIND OF COMPLICATION IN A RELATIONSHIP.
"NOT TO MENTION A BABY FATHERED BY JACKIE ESTACADO.
COME HERE, SWEETIE...
...YOU'RE OKAY...
...YOU'RE FINE.
"DO YOU LOVE SARA?"
"I THINK THAT'S... REALLY BETWEEN ME AND YOUR SISTER."
"IT'S COOL..."

...I'M NOT TRYING TO PRY INTO WHAT YOU TWO HAVE. JUST CURIOUS.
THERE... ALL CLEAN AGAIN.
DUNNO WHAT WE'RE GONNA DO WITH YOU WHEN YOU GET TOO BIG FOR THE SINK.
GEEBL!
SPLISH
THANKS, ALWAYS NICE TO BE INCLUDED.
SPLASH
BREEP BREEP
HEY, WHERE ARE YOU?
NO, EVERYTHING'S GOOD. JULIE JUST GOT DONE GIVING HOPE HER BATH.
YEAH, GOT BOTH OF US WET, ACTUALLY. SO YOU ON YOUR WAY HOME NOW?
OH, OKAY, GO DO WHAT YOU HAVE TO DO.
TELL HER I SAID GOODBYE AND GOOD LUCK, OKAY?
SEE YOU THEN. BYE.
SARA SAID SOMETHING HELD HER UP, SO SHE'S HEADING STRAIGHT OVER TO SEE DANI NOW, BEFORE SHE LEAVES TOWN.
GRAB THAT TOWEL, WOULD YOU? LET'S GET SQUIRMY HERE DRIED OFF.
THANKS.
THAT'S KIND OF A WEIRD FRIENDSHIP, ISN'T IT? I MEAN...

"...DIDN'T SARA TRY TO KILL HER?"
THANKS FOR COMING.

OF COURSE I CAME. YOU THINK I'D LET YOU LEAVE TOWN BEFORE I GOT TO SEE YOU?
I'M STILL NOT EVEN SURE WHY YOU'RE GOING. WOULDN'T IT MAKE MORE SENSE TO STAY HERE...

...WHERE I CAN MAYBE HELP YOU, INSTEAD OF GOING BACK TO NEW ORLEANS?

IT'S TEMPTING... BUT I FEEL LIKE I NEED A FRESH START.

THIS SEEMS BEST, AT LEAST UNTIL I CAN GET MY BEARINGS WITH EVERYTHING.

"I USED TO THINK IT WAS DUMB LUCK OR SHEER COINCIDENCE THAT THEY EVER EVEN MET. SARA ENDED UP PASSING ON THE WITCHBLADE TO DANI WHEN SHE FOUND OUT SHE WAS PREGNANT...

"...THEN GOT HALF OF IT BACK AFTER SHE HAD HOPE. AND WE KNOW HOW THAT EVENTUALLY TURNED OUT.

AND FINCH IS GOING WITH YOU?
YEAH, WE'RE GOING TO SEE WHAT THIS THING WITH US IS...IF IT'S EVEN A THING.

LOTS OF QUESTIONS, NOT SO MANY ANSWERS, SARA.
BUT I THINK I HAVE A BETTER CHANCE OF FINDING THEM IN A PLACE THAT FEELS LIKE HOME.
"NOW IT SEEMS LIKE IT ALL HAPPENED FOR A REASON."

DO YOU MISS IT? THE WITCHBLADE?
NOT REALLY. I STILL SENSE A CONNECTION TO IT...
...BUT IT'S NOT PART OF ME, IF THAT MAKES ANY SENSE.
MAYBE THE WITCHBLADE WAS JUST SUPPOSED TO BE A STEPPING STONE FOR ME, SOMETHING ALONG THE WAY...
...TO HELP GET ME READY FOR WHAT I'M SUPPOSED TO BE DOING.
"AND NOW DANI IS THE ANGELUS? OR THE ANGELUS IS HER? OR SOMETHING?
"I DON'T REALLY GET HOW ALL THIS WORKS."
"GUESS YOUR SISTER DIDN'T FILL YOU IN VERY MUCH ON THE DETAILS, DID SHE?"

I HAVE TO ADMIT, LOOKS GOOD ON YOU.

FEELS GOOD.

"DON'T QUOTE ME ON ANY OF THIS, IT'S JUST WHAT I'VE PICKED UP FROM SARA. SHE'S THE ONE WHO ***LIVES*** IT, I'M ONLY A ***BYSTANDER.***

"THE ANGELUS IS ONE OF THE PRIMAL FORCES OF THE UNIVERSE, THE EMBODIMENT OF ***LIGHT,*** RIVAL TO THE DARKNESS. ***BOTH*** TAKE HUMAN HOSTS.

"THE WAY SARA EXPLAINED IT, THE DARKNESS SEEMS TO LET ITS HOSTS RETAIN A MEASURE OF ***FREE WILL,*** WHILE THE ANGELUS WANTS ***PUPPETS.***

"AND THE DARKNESS USUALLY KICKS THE ANGELUS' ASS.

AND IT STILL FEELS LIKE ***ME.***
"SO LOOKS LIKE THE ANGELUS IS FINALLY TRYING A DIFFERENT STRATEGY.
IS ***THAT*** SUPPOSED TO HAPPEN?

REACTING BECAUSE ***MOM*** IS AROUND, I SUPPOSE.
"DANI'S GOING TO BE MORE OF A ***CO-PILOT*** THAN A ***PASSENGER.***

"SHE'S REALLY GOING TO BE LEAVING HER OLD LIFE BEHIND."
"SOUNDS LIKE A PLAN. THERE'S A LOT *I* WANT TO PUT BEHIND ME-- GETTING BUSTED FOR DRUGS AND GOING TO JAIL ARE JUST THE *TOP* OF THE LIST.
"SARA'S HELPING ME DO THAT. I DIDN'T *REALIZE* IT AT THE TIME, BUT SHE WAS HELPING ME DO THAT EVEN WHEN I GOT ARRESTED.
IF YOU NEED ME... FOR ANYTHING, ANY TIME... YOU LET ME KNOW.
I WILL.
ABSOLUTELY I WILL.
I DON'T THINK YOU TWO HAVE EVER BEEN OFFICIALLY INTRODUCED.
FINCH, THIS IS *SARA.*
SARA, *FINCH.*
IT'S GOOD TO FINALLY MEET YOU.
YOU TOO. LISTEN, YOU TAKE *GOOD CARE* OF HER, OKAY?
COUNT ON IT.
BYE, SARA.
BYE...
"I'M GLAD WE HAD A CHANCE TO TALK, GLEASON. SARA'S MY SISTER, BUT SOMETIMES SHE FEELS PRETTY *DISTANT.* THIS HELPS."
"WELL, YOU WANT HELP, YOU ASK A *COP,* RIGHT?"
"LISTEN, CAN YOU FINISH GETTING HER INTO HER PAJAMAS WHILE I CHANGE? THE SHIRT'S STILL PRETTY *SOAKED.*"
"SURE THING."
*EDITOR'S NOTE: FOLLOW DANI'S ADVENTURES IN THE *ANGELUS* TRADE PAPERBACK AVAILABLE NOW! -FILIP & PHIL

COME ON, JAMMIES ON, THEN MOMMY SHOULD BE HERE PRETTY SOON.
BWEEBWAH

OH, GOOD, I WAS AFRAID SHE'D BE ASLEEP ALREADY.
HI, SWEETIE.

WERE YOU A GOOD GIRL FOR AUNTIE JULES?
MMMAAAA!

SHE WAS VERY GOOD...EXCEPT FOR DINNER TIME.
YAYAA!
C'MERE, YOU LITTLE MONKEY.

YOU DO A GREAT JOB LOOKING AFTER HER. I REALLY APPRECIATE IT, JULES.
HEY, IT'S MY JOB... UNTIL I CAN FIND A JOB.

THANKS FOR FEEDING HER. DID SHE EAT PRETTY WELL?
WE MANAGED TO GET ***SOME*** OF IT IN HER MOUTH.
AND I'M HAPPY TO DO IT. I HEARD MY BIG SISTER USED TO FEED ***ME*** WHEN I WAS A BABY.

LOOK, I KNOW WE STILL HAVE A LOT OF GROUND TO COVER. EVERYTHING'S BEEN A LITTLE ***CRAZY*** SINCE YOU GOT HERE...
I WISH I COULD TELL YOU THINGS WILL GET BACK TO NORMAL, BUT THERE'S NOT MUCH "NORMAL" IN MY LIFE.

THERE'S JUST ***ROLL WITH*** WHATEVER COMES NEXT.
I CAN ROLL.

I'M GLAD YOU'RE HERE, JULES.
ME TOO, SIS.

SO MY ***BOYFRIEND*** WAS SUPPOSED TO BE BRINGING GROCERIES. WHAT'D YOU DO WITH HIM?
YOU MEAN ***BEFORE*** OR ***AFTER*** WE HAD SEX ON THE KITCHEN TABLE?
THAT'S NICE TALK AROUND YOUR NIECE.

I SEE THE HOT OLDER SISTER FINALLY SHOWED UP?
AND SHE HEARD YOU WERE TAKING ADVANTAGE OF HER *INNOCENT* YOUNGER SISTER.
I HAVE NOTHING TO SAY. I'M NOT THE *KISS-AND-TELL* TYPE.
HERE... I'LL GET HER SETTLED DOWN WHILE YOU TWO TALK. COME ON IN AND SAY GOODNIGHT WHEN YOU'RE READY.
THANKS, JULES.
SORRY I'M LATE.
ANYTHING A LITTLE *OUT OF THE ORDINARY* HAPPEN ON YOUR RUN?
OUT OF THE ORDINARY FOR *ME,* OR OUT OF THE ORDINARY FOR EVERYBODY ELSE?
YOU'RE RIGHT, I PROBABLY DON'T WANT TO KNOW.
COME ON, DON'T BE LIKE THAT. I'M SORRY THINGS HAVE BEEN...THE WAY THEY'VE BEEN.
BUT YOU KNEW I CAME WITH BAGGAGE WHEN WE *STARTED* THIS.
BAGS MARKED "TURNS EVIL" AND "NEARLY KILLS HER FRIEND"? I DON'T THINK I GOT THAT MEMO.

ALL THAT'S OVER, GLEASON. I PROMISE.
IS THAT A PROMISE YOU CAN KEEP?

I KNOW THERE'S STILL A LOT WE NEED TO WORK ON. A LOT I NEED TO MAKE UP FOR.
BUT THERE'S TIME TO DO THAT, ISN'T THERE?

TELL ME THERE'S TIME.
PLEASE?

THERE'S TIME.

GOOD.

HELLO?
IS ANYONE HERE?
I'M BACK.
I KNOW I'VE BEEN GONE A WHILE, BUT I WANT TO MAKE THINGS RIGHT.
YOU'VE BEEN LOST FOR A TIME.
THERE WERE THOSE OF US WHO WONDERED IF YOU WOULD EVER RETURN.
BUT YOU FOUND YOUR WAY AGAIN.
I... HAD SOME HELP.

WE'VE BEEN WAITING FOR YOU, SARA.
WELCOME HOME...

WITCHBLADE® REDEMPTION

"The Bridge" part 1

HELLO?
IS ANYBODY THERE?

LIQUOR STORE IN TOWN WAS JUST CLOSING, BUT I WAS ABLE TO TALK THEM INTO STAYING OPEN FOR A COUPLE MORE MINUTES.
NOT A *HUGE* SELECTION, BUT THEN AGAIN, WHAT DO *I* KNOW? IF IT DOESN'T HAVE A *HEAD* ON IT, IT'S BEYOND MY EXPERTISE.
SHIRAZ IS OKAY, RIGHT?
SHIT... I FORGOT TO GET A *CORKSCREW.*
DON'T WORRY ABOUT IT...

...I'VE GOT IT COVERED.
YOU JUST COME ON OVER HERE, GLEASON, AND *I'LL* TAKE CARE OF YOU.

YOU KNOW, WHEN YOU SENT ME OUT FOR A BOTTLE OF WINE, I WAS DUMB ENOUGH TO THINK IT WAS BECAUSE YOU ACTUALLY WANTED A BOTTLE OF WINE...
...NOT SO YOU COULD GET NAKED.
IS THAT A COMPLAINT?
NO, MA'AM.
GOOD, NOW GIVE ME THAT THING.
YOU ARE TALKING ABOUT THE BOTTLE, RIGHT?
FOR NOW.
WE GET MY SISTER TO WATCH THE BABY FOR THE WEEKEND...

...YOU TAKE ME ALL THE WAY TO VERMONT, I EXPECT A LITTLE ROMANCE.
I WANT TO GET BACK TO WHERE WE WERE BEFORE... EVERYTHING THAT HAPPENED.

I'LL DEFINITELY DRINK TO THAT. HOW 'BOUT YOU, DETECTIVE GLEASON?

I'M IRISH, WE DRINK TO DAMN NEAR ANYTHING.
BUT?
I CAN TELL THERE'S A "BUT," EVEN IF YOU DIDN'T SAY IT.

YEAH, I GUESS THERE IS.
I'M... NOT SO SURE HOW EASY IT'S GOING TO BE TO JUST HIT REWIND. A LOT HAPPENED, SARA.
IF I COULD TAKE ANY OF IT BACK, I WOULD. BUT I KNOW IT DOESN'T WORK LIKE THAT.
IT WASN'T REALLY ME, BUT AT THE SAME TIME IT WAS. I'M NOT GOING TO TRY TO CONVINCE YOU OF SOME BULLSHIT COP-OUT EXCUSE LIKE I WAS MIND-CONTROLLED.

I DID THOSE THINGS. I SAID THOSE THINGS.
IT'S NOT VERY OFTEN YOU HAVE THAT SIDE OF YOURSELF EXPOSED...MUCH LESS HAVE TO STARE IT IN THE FACE.
I HURT YOU, I HURT DANI, I HURT EVERYONE. I CAN'T PRETEND IT DIDN'T HAPPEN. IT'S GOING TO STAY WITH ME.

SO THE BEST I CAN DO IS TRY TO MAKE UP FOR IT...IF YOU'LL LET ME.
I DIDN'T WALK AWAY WHEN I FOUND OUT YOU WERE PREGNANT.

I'M GENERALLY A GLASS HALF-FULL GUY. BUT THIS HASN'T BEEN EASY.

YOU SAID SOME THINGS...
I KNOW WHAT I SAID.
JACKIE ESTACADO IS HOPE'S FATHER. HE'S ALWAYS GOING TO BE HOPE'S FATHER.

NOT EXACTLY WHO I WOULD'VE PICKED TO BE MY BABY DADDY, BUT IT IS WHAT IT IS.
I NEED YOU TO UNDERSTAND THAT JACKIE...WHO HE IS, WHAT HE IS...DOESN'T MEAN ANYTHING TO ME.

NOT LIKE YOU DO.
I'M NOT EXACTLY A TEENAGER ANYMORE, YOU KNOW? I'VE FIGURED OUT THAT THE BAD BOYS MIGHT BE THE ONES WHO GET YOUR MOTOR REVVING, BUT THAT'S ABOUT ALL THEY DO.
I'VE GROWN UP ENOUGH TO REALIZE THAT I WANT A GOOD MAN, NOT A BAD BOY. AND YOU'RE A GOOD MAN, PATRICK GLEASON.

FOR A WHILE... I KNEW THIS WAS GOOD, BUT I DIDN'T KNOW IF IT WAS RIGHT.
I GUESS I WANTED TO HEAR BELLS AND WHISTLES GO OFF AND TELL ME YOU WERE THE ONE.

BUT NOW I KNOW THAT DOESN'T ALWAYS HAPPEN. SOMETIMES IT SNEAKS UP ON YOU.
LOOK, IT'S NOT EASY FOR ME TO LET ANYONE INTO THIS LIFE I HAVE. AND THE PEOPLE I CARE ABOUT THE MOST ARE THE HARDEST TO LET IN, BECAUSE OF WHAT MIGHT HAPPEN.

BUT YOU'RE THE ONE I WANT TO BE WITH.

YOU'RE THE ONE I LOVE.

THIS IS THE PART WHERE YOU SAY IT BACK.
THERE WERE TIMES I'VE WANTED TO SAY IT.

BUT I NEVER DID BECAUSE I FELT LIKE I DIDN'T KNOW WHAT WOULD BE COMING BACK THE OTHER WAY.
WE WERE TOGETHER, BUT I DIDN'T KNOW IF YOU FELT THE SAME WAY.

I LOVE YOU TOO, SARA.

I GUESS I WILL DRINK TO THAT.

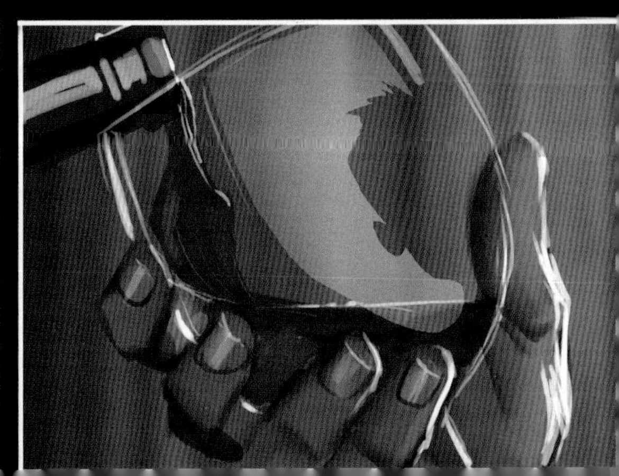

TO US.
I LIKE THAT.
KLINK
MMMM...
...YOU'RE OVERDRESSED.

THAT'S A ***SCHOOL.*** LOOKS LIKE ***BOTH*** THE SHERIFF AND STATE TROOPERS.
THAT KIND OF PRESENCE, SOMETHING'S GOING ON. NOT A ***GOOD*** SOMETHING.
WE'RE SUPPOSED TO BE ON ***VACATION.***

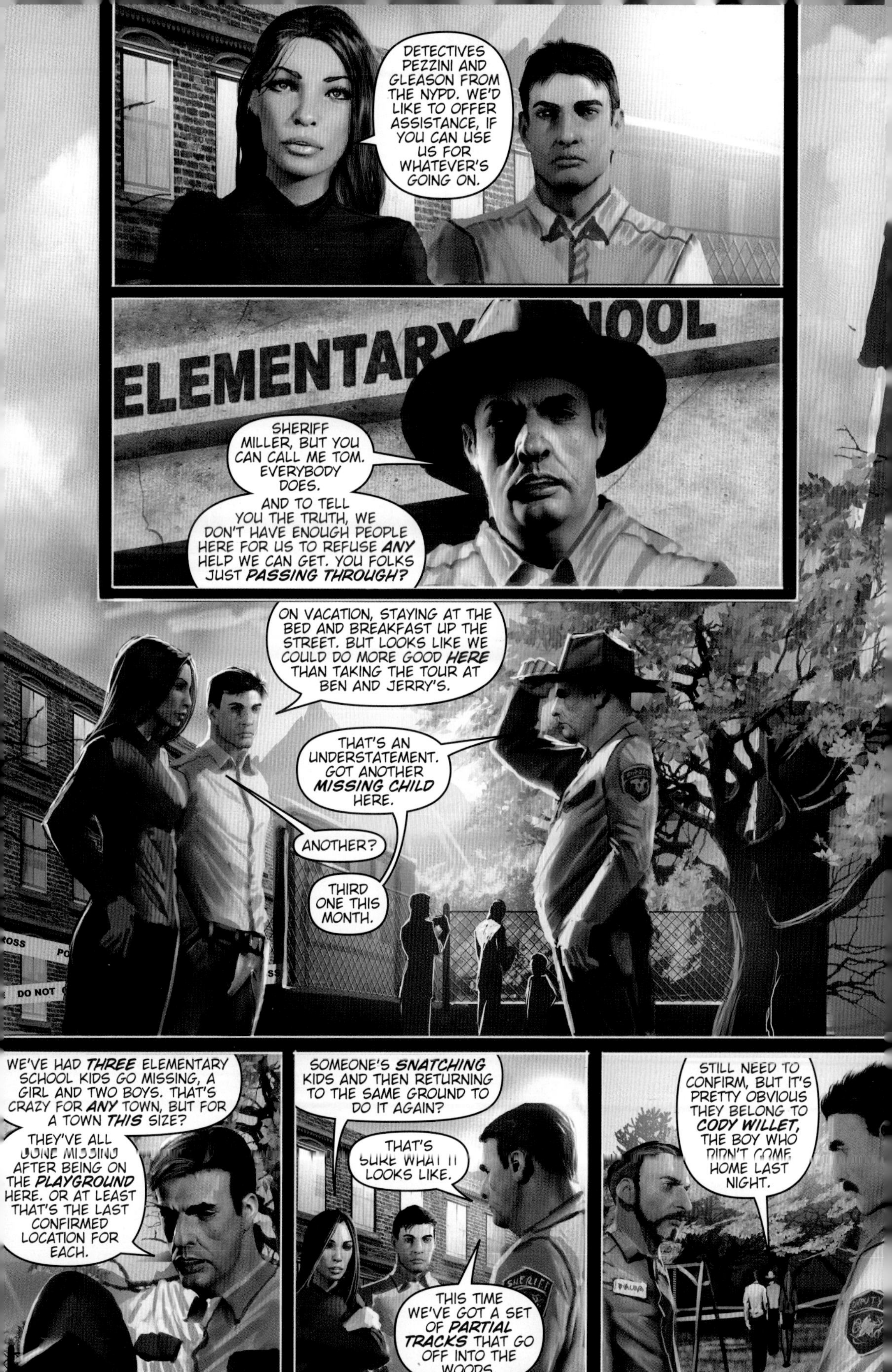

DETECTIVES PEZZINI AND GLEASON FROM THE NYPD. WE'D LIKE TO OFFER ASSISTANCE, IF YOU CAN USE US FOR WHATEVER'S GOING ON.
ELEMENTARY
SHERIFF MILLER, BUT YOU CAN CALL ME TOM. EVERYBODY DOES.
AND TO TELL YOU THE TRUTH, WE DON'T HAVE ENOUGH PEOPLE HERE FOR US TO REFUSE ANY HELP WE CAN GET. YOU FOLKS JUST PASSING THROUGH?
ON VACATION, STAYING AT THE BED AND BREAKFAST UP THE STREET. BUT LOOKS LIKE WE COULD DO MORE GOOD HERE THAN TAKING THE TOUR AT BEN AND JERRY'S.
THAT'S AN UNDERSTATEMENT. GOT ANOTHER MISSING CHILD HERE.
ANOTHER?
THIRD ONE THIS MONTH.
DO NOT
WE'VE HAD THREE ELEMENTARY SCHOOL KIDS GO MISSING, A GIRL AND TWO BOYS. THAT'S CRAZY FOR ANY TOWN, BUT FOR A TOWN THIS SIZE?
THEY'VE ALL GONE MISSING AFTER BEING ON THE PLAYGROUND HERE. OR AT LEAST THAT'S THE LAST CONFIRMED LOCATION FOR EACH.
SOMEONE'S SNATCHING KIDS AND THEN RETURNING TO THE SAME GROUND TO DO IT AGAIN?
THAT'S SURE WHAT IT LOOKS LIKE.
THIS TIME WE'VE GOT A SET OF PARTIAL TRACKS THAT GO OFF INTO THE WOODS.
STILL NEED TO CONFIRM, BUT IT'S PRETTY OBVIOUS THEY BELONG TO CODY WILLET, THE BOY WHO DIDN'T COME HOME LAST NIGHT.

WE'LL GET YOU THE FILES ON ALL THREE KIDS THAT ARE MISSING.
HAVE YOU HAD DOGS OUT?
FIRST THING. HERE'S ANOTHER NOW.
AIN'T NORMAL, THOUGH. ANY OF THE DOGS WE'VE HAD OUT HERE, THEY GET A WAYS DOWN THE TRAIL, THEN TURN TAIL AND COME BACK.
SAME THING?
JUST LIKE THE REST.
YOU'RE A GOOD BOY, HUH? SURE YOU ARE.
WHAT'S OUT THERE, BOY?
SOMETHING THAT SCARES YOU?
HE'S SPOOKED, THAT MUCH IS OBVIOUS.
BEFORE THIS, I'VE NEVER SEEN HIM GET SPOOKED BY ANYTHING.

THERE'S SOMETHING IN THESE WOODS THE DOGS DON'T LIKE.
WELL, I'LL TELL YOU WHAT'S NOT IN THESE WOODS, AND THAT'S THOSE THREE KIDS. THE TRACKS EVENTUALLY PETER OUT, LIKE THE KIDS JUST UP AND VANISHED.
I KNOW THIS AIN'T EXACTLY MANHATTAN, BUT IF EITHER OF YOU HAS AN IDEA, WE'RE WILLING TO WALK DOWN ANY PATH THAT MIGHT LEAD TO SOMETHING.
NOT IMMEDIATELY. WITH THE KIND OF CASES WE USUALLY HANDLE, THE RIGHT ANSWER ISN'T ALWAYS THE MOST OBVIOUS ONE.
IF IT'S ALL RIGHT WITH YOU, SHERIFF, WE'LL HELP WITH THE SEARCH, AND THEN WE'D LIKE TO LOOK AROUND A LITTLE MORE, SEE IF SOMETHING JUMPS OUT AT US.
SURE THING...BUT YOU KNOW HOW THIS WORKS. CLOCK'S TICKING FOR CODY.
GLEASON, WHATEVER WE FIND...

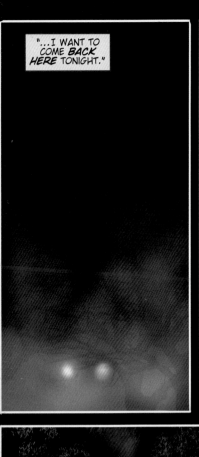
"...I WANT TO COME BACK HERE TONIGHT."

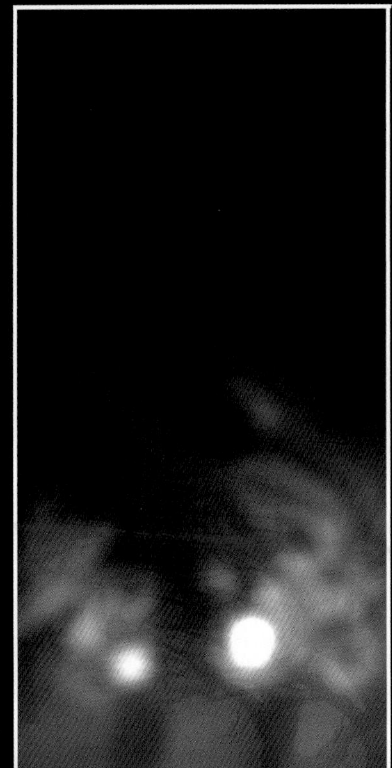

IT'S QUIET.
WE'RE IN THE MIDDLE OF THE WOODS IN VERMONT. OF COURSE IT'S QUIET.

I MEAN I'M A CITY BOY. IF IT'S THE MIDDLE OF THE NIGHT AND I CAN'T HEAR A FEW SIRENS, AND MAYBE SOME SANITATION WORKERS DESTROYING GARBAGE CANS, IT CREEPS ME OUT.
DIDN'T ANYBODY EVER TELL YOU THAT THERE'S NOTHING IN THE DARK THAT'S NOT THERE IN THE LIGHT?

YEAH, THEN I STARTED HANGING AROUND WITH YOU AND FIGURED OUT THAT WAS ALL BULLSHIT.
YOU HAVE EVEN A GUESS AS TO WHAT WE'RE LOOKING FOR?
BESIDES MISSING KIDS? NOT SURE.
SOMETHING JUST FEELS... OFF...ABOUT THIS PLACE.

"WHO'S THAT TRIP-TRAPPING OVER MY ***BRIDGE?"***

CUTE.

YOU KNOW, SOMETHING LIKE THIS...

...I CAN'T HELP BUT THINK HOW I'D FEEL IF ***HOPE*** WAS EVER MISSING.

WAIT, YOU ***HEAR*** THAT?

UH... HEAR ***WHAT?***

...JUST IN CASE.
HEY, GLEASON, DON'T GET TOO FAR, SOMETHING'S...
GLEASON?
WHERE'D YOU GO?
COME ON, DAMN IT, THIS ISN'T FUNNY!
I TAKE BACK WHAT I SAID ABOUT YOU BEING A GOOD MAN...

GLEASON!
ANSWER ME!
HNNGH...

SPAASH

GUESS THERE'S NO SENSE IN READING YOU YOUR *RIGHTS...*

GHNN!
UHNFF...

WITCHBLADE
REDEMPTION

"The Bridge" part 2

MISTER?
HEY, MISTER?
YOU'D BETTER WAKE UP...
...HE'LL BE BACK SOON.
WHO'LL BE BACK... WHERE...?
...WHERE... AM I? I WAS IN THE WOODS AND THEN...
...I GUESS MAYBE I FELL, BECAUSE I REMEMBER HITTING MY HEAD, BUT NOT...

...NOT HOW I ENDED UP *HERE.*
WHAT *IS* THIS? I BUMPED MY HEAD AND WOKE UP IN GOD DAMN *MIDDLE EARTH?*

WAIT...YOU KIDS, *YOU'RE* THE ONES WHO DISAPPEARED IN THE WOODS, AREN'T YOU?
WHICH ONE OF YOU IS *CODY?*
I AM...BUT I WOULDN'T SAY WE *DISAPPEARED.*

WE'VE BEEN HANGING OUT HERE. YOU KNOW, 'TIL IT'S *SAFE.*
YEAH, JUST 'TIL IT'S SAFE.

WHAT'S *THAT* MEAN?
AND WHERE EXACTLY *IS* THIS PLACE? HOW'D YOU EVEN *FIND* IT? I DON'T UNDERSTAND WHAT'S...

WHUMP
NOW WHAT?

JEEZUS!
SARA!

WHAT'S THE MATTER?
NOT USED TO SOMEONE WHO *FIGHTS BACK?*
DON'T BE *SCARED*...
...JUST STAY BEHIND ME.
UHFF!
GOOD JOB.
NOW I'M PISSED.

HNNF
AARGH!
GET BACK HERE!
DON'T!

GET OUT OF THE *WAY,* KID!
DON'T HURT HIM!
WHAT?

ARE YOU ALL RIGHT? THAT LOOKS LIKE IT *HURTS.*
IT HURTS.
BUT I WILL HEAL.
WHY DID THE LADY HURT YOU?

WHAT THE *HELL* IS GOING ON HERE?
BELIEVE ME, I'M STILL TRYING TO SORT THAT OUT.

YOU OKAY, GLEASON?
ASIDE FROM BEING CONFUSED AS SHIT, *FINE.*

THOSE ARE THE MISSING KIDS?

APPARENTLY NOT ANY WORSE FROM THE EXPERIENCE. WHAT HIS STORY IS, OR WHAT HE'S DOING WITH THE KIDS, I CAN'T BEGIN TO GUESS.

BUT HE DIDN'T EAT ME, SO THAT EARNS HIM SOME POINTS RIGHT THERE.

THE CHILDREN ARE UNDER MY PROTECTION.

AND I HAVE NOT EATEN A HUMAN... IN A VERY LONG TIME.

WHAT ARE YOU? WHAT'S... THIS?

THIS IS WHERE I LIVE.

IN THE UNDERNEATH, IN THE SHADOWS UNDER THE WORLD.

"...BUT THAT WAS LONG AGO.

"THERE WERE *WONDERS* THEN. MY PEOPLE AND THE OTHER CREATURES OF THE ANCIENT WORLD WERE PLENTIFUL.

"BUT THE WORLD MOVED ON. BIT BY BIT, CENTURY AFTER CENTURY, THE WORLD OF MEN GREW **STRONGER**, AND OUR WORLD RECEDED.

"THE *MAGIC* WENT AWAY.

"ENCHANTMENT WAS SACRIFICED FOR THE MUNDANE, AND WE FADED AWAY.
"THE FEW OF US WHO REMAINED WERE FORCED TO HIDE..."

...CLINGING TO THE SHADOWS OF YOUR GRAY AND BARREN WORLD.
YOU UNDERSTAND WHAT HAS BEEN LOST.
YOU BEAR ONE OF THE ANCIENT POWERS, OLDER EVEN THAN MY PEOPLE. WE FOUGHT BESIDE IT LONG AGO.

YEAH, WELL, I'M NOT THE FIRST ONE TO HAVE THIS. I CERTAINLY WON'T BE THE LAST.
NONE OF WHICH EXPLAINS WHAT THESE KIDS ARE DOING HERE.

ESPECIALLY FOR THREE WEEKS FOR SOME OF YOU. I CAN'T IMAGINE WHAT YOUR PARENTS ARE GOING THROUGH.
THREE WEEKS?

THREE WEEKS? NO, THAT'S NOT RIGHT.
WE'VE ONLY BEEN HERE A COUPLE HOURS. UNTIL IT'S SAFE AGAIN.

WHY DO YOU SAY "UNTIL IT'S SAFE?" SAFE FROM WHAT?
NOT SUPPOSED TO TELL.

YOU CAN TELL ME. I'M A POLICE OFFICER.

WELL... SAFE FROM **LEON.**
WHO'S LEON?
THE JANITOR AT SCHOOL. HE'S **CREEPY.** ALL THE KIDS KNOW IT. WE TRY TO STAY AWAY FROM HIM, BUT SOMETIMES...
...SOMETIMES HE **TOUCHES** KIDS. WHEN HE **CAN.** I THINK HE EVEN TOOK A KID AWAY A LONG TIME AGO.
LEON SAYS NO ONE CAN EVER TELL, OR OUR PARENTS WON'T **WANT** US ANYMORE.
YOU'RE **SURE** THIS LEON DOES THESE THINGS? YOU'RE **ABSOLUTELY** SURE?
UH-HUH.

THEY KNOW THEY CAN COME HERE AND BE **SAFE.** I HIDE THEM IN THE UNDERNEATH, JUST AS I HIDE MYSELF.
TIME IN MY WORLD IS **DIFFERENT** THAN IN YOURS. **HOURS** HAVE PASSED FOR THEM HERE, YET IN YOUR WORLD... MUCH MORE.
WE HAVE TO GET THEM **HOME.** EVERYONE THINKS...WELL, THEY THINK THE **WORST.**

BUT WE **LIKE IT** HERE.
I KNOW, BUT YOUR PARENTS ARE SO **WORRIED.**
I PROMISE YOU'LL BE **SAFE.** YOU WON'T HAVE TO WORRY ABOUT **ANYONE** HURTING YOU.

HOW ARE WE GOING TO **EXPLAIN** THIS? "TROLL UNDER THE BRIDGE" ISN'T EXACTLY THE MOST BELIEVABLE STORY, DESPITE IT BEING THE **TRUTH.**
WE'LL SAY THEY WERE LOST IN THE WOODS. IT'S **CREDIBLE,** AND EVERYBODY WILL BE SO RELIEVED THEY WON'T ASK TOO MANY QUESTIONS.

WE HAVE TO **GO.** TIME TO SAY YOUR GOODBYES.
BE GOOD.
BE BRAVE.
THE MAGIC IS NOT YET LOST TO YOU.
WE'LL MISS YOU.
WE'LL MISS YOU BECAUSE WE LOVE YOU.
CAN WE COME BACK?

THIS IS FAR ENOUGH.

I CALLED THE SHERIFF, HE'S BRINGING EVERYONE'S PARENTS UP HERE.
WE CAN JUST *WAIT* FOR THEM.

SEEMS LIKE THEY'VE ALL GOT THEIR *STORIES* DOWN. "LOST IN THE WOODS" AND ALL THAT.
JUST MAKE SURE YOU KEEP THE SHERIFF AND THE STATE TROOPERS OCCUPIED.

KEEP THEM OCCUPIED *LONG ENOUGH* FOR ME TO DO WHAT I NEED TO DO.

NICE SEEING THE KIDS REUNITED WITH THEIR FAMILIES...
...ISN'T IT?
WHO...
...WHO ARE YOU?

MY NAME'S SARA. I'M A DETECTIVE WITH THE NYPD.
BUT THAT DOESN'T REALLY MATTER.
HOW DID YOU GET IN HERE? THE SCHOOL'S NOT OPEN YET, YOU'RE NOT SUPPOSED TO BE HERE.

WHAT DO YOU WANT?
I WANT TO TALK.

WE CAN... YOU CAN TALK TO ME FROM OVER THERE.

I WANT TO ASK YOU ABOUT THE ***CHILDREN,*** LEON. YOU KNOW WHICH CHILDREN I MEAN.
YOU NEED TO GET AWAY FROM ME!
THAT'S NOT GOING TO HAPPEN.

LEAVE ME ALONE!
CLANK

THE CHILDREN ARE ***SCARED*** OF YOU, LEON. THEY THINK YOU'RE SOME KIND OF ***THREAT.***
I THINK MAYBE THEY'RE ***RIGHT.***
NO!

THEY'RE JUST ***MAKING IT UP!***
DON'T ***LIE*** TO ME, LEON.

TELL ME THE ***TRUTH!***
YES!

YES, YEARS AGO I ***TOOK*** ONE OF THEM!
THE LITTLE ONES, IT'S SO ***HARD*** FOR ME TO KEEP MY HANDS OFF THEM. BUT IT WAS JUST THE ONE. THE REST...

...THE REST KNOW WHERE TO ***HIDE.***

WHAT ARE YOU GOING TO ***DO*** TO ME?

WHERE ARE YOU ***TAKING*** ME?
WHY DID YOU KEEP ME ***LOCKED AWAY*** ALL DAY?

ANSWER ME!
YOU'RE THE POLICE! YOU'RE SUPPOSED TO ARREST ME, YOU'RE NOT SUPPOSED TO DO THIS!

I'M NOT GOING TO DO ANYTHING.

YOU CAN'T JUST ***SHOOT ME*** OUT HERE!
YOU'D NEVER ***GET AWAY*** WITH IT!

SOMEONE WILL KNOW! THEY'LL EVENTUALLY FIND MY BODY!
PLEASE!

WAIT... WHAT'RE YOU **DOING?**
YOU'RE JUST **LEAVING** ME?
I WON'T TELL, YOU KNOW. I WON'T TELL **ANYONE.** I'LL **NEVER** TOUCH A KID AGAIN!

HWAAGH!

GHHAAAAA

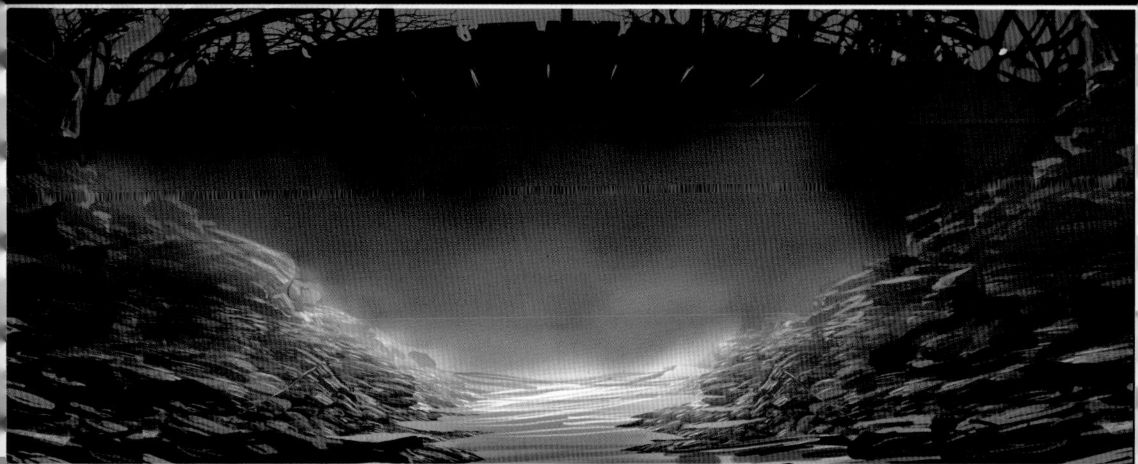

"COME ON, COME ON, WHERE THE HELL ARE YOU? IF YOU DON'T GET HERE NOW..."
...AND I MEAN RIGHT NOW, I WON'T MAKE IT OUT OF HERE.
AND YOU WON'T GET WHAT YOU WANT.
SLAMM
OH GOD...
...OH GOD...
...PLEASE...

SO HURRY THE HELL UP! **SHE'S** ON HER WAY, I KNOW SHE IS.
SHE'LL **KILL ME** LIKE SHE'S SQUASHING A GOD DAMN BUG. DO YOU HAVE **ANY IDEA** THE NUMBER OF PEOPLE WHO HAVE DIED ALREADY?
WHO **GIVES** A SHIT ABOUT THE **MONEY?** I WON'T BE ABLE TO **SPEND** IT IF I'M **DEAD.** NOW HURRY UP!
YOU'VE BEEN VERY **NAUGHTY,** DR. SINGH, TAKING THINGS THAT DON'T BELONG TO YOU.

YOU SHOULD HAVE JUST COME HOME WHEN YOU HAD THE CHANCE.
HERE, YOU CAN HAVE IT BACK!
YOU CAN JUST TAKE IT AND LET ME GO, APHRODITE. PLEASE...
YOU KNOW THAT WON'T WORK, DR. SINGH. YOU HELPED BUILD ME.
BRAKKA BRAKKA BRAKKA
CD 0018
MOVE YOUR ASS, DOCTOR.
PULL ME UP! HURRY!

BITCH WON'T BE WALKING AWAY FROM THAT.
ARE YOU STUPID? THAT'S APHRODITE IV.
YOU MIGHT SLOW HER DOWN...
"...BUT YOU CAN'T STOP HER."

WITCHBLADE® REDEMPTION

"Almost Human" part 1

I
II
I JUST ARRIVED, WHAT'S HER STATUS?
AND SHE MADE IT BACK HERE UNDER HER OWN POWER?
WHAT ABOUT SINGH? SHE DIDN'T GET TO HIM IN TIME?

III
IV
THAT SON OF A BITCH KNOWS EVERYTHING! ALL OUR WORK, AND NOW HE'S SELLING IT TO THEM!
WE SHOULD HAVE KILLED HIM MONTHS AGO WHEN WE HAD THE OPPORTUNITY.
NO, YOU WEREN'T SURE! I DIDN'T TRUST HIM FROM THE FIRST.
HANG ON...

...I'M COMING IN.

IS SHE GOING TO ***MAKE IT?***

WE'VE ***STABILIZED*** HER, BUT SHE'S TAKEN A LOT OF DAMAGE.

THE NEURAL NET WAS COMPROMISED, WE'LL HAVE TO REPLACE PORTIONS OF THE CHASSIS AND NEARLY ***ALL*** OF THE SNYTH-SKIN.

AND EVEN WHEN ALL ***THAT'S*** COMPLETED, WE'LL HAVE TO RUN A FULL DIAGNOSTIC BEFORE SHE GOES BACK INTO THE FIELD.

NO TIME. WE NEED TO SEND HER BACK OUT AS SOON AS SHE'S FUNCTIONAL.
I'LL SAY THIS FOR HER...

...NONE OF THE PREVIOUS MODELS WOULD'VE EVEN BEEN IN ONE PIECE AFTER SUFFERING THIS KIND OF DAMAGE.
DON'T WORRY, ONCE WE HAVE HER PATCHED UP, APHRODITE IV IS GOING TO DO EXACTLY WHAT WE CREATED HER FOR...
...GO KILL SOMEONE.

UNLESS I'M MISSING SOMETHING...
...THERE ARE NO IDENTIFYING MARKS.
NOTHING AT ALL.
BUT SOMEBODY SURE USED A HELL OF A LOT OF FIREPOWER UP HERE.
SARA? YOU COME UP WITH ANYTHING?
WELL, NOBODY DROPPED A BUSINESS CARD, IF THAT'S WHAT YOU'RE ASKING, GLEASON.

BUT I CAN TELL YOU THAT WHOEVER CAME THROUGH THIS DOOR HAS BEEN WORKING OUT.
THAT, OR WE'RE TALKING 'ROID RAGE THAT'D MAKE ROGER CLEMENS JEALOUS.
DAMN THING'S TORN RIGHT OFF THE HINGES.
WHAT ABOUT YOU?
JUST SOME GUESSES THAT DON'T REALLY ADD UP. WE'LL HAVE TO WAIT UNTIL BALLISTICS GETS HERE AND PULLS THE SLUGS...
...BUT LOOKS LIKE THE TRAJECTORY CAME FROM ABOVE. LARGE-CALIBER WEAPON, TOO, LARGE ENOUGH THAT YOU COULDN'T CARRY IT AROUND COMFORTABLY.
SO HOW DID THAT HAPPEN? ANGLE IS WRONG FOR ANY OF THE SURROUNDING BUILDINGS.
IT'S A LITTLE CURIOUS, BUT NOT EXACTLY THE SORT OF THING WE GET CALLED ABOUT.
YEAH, SPECIAL CASES IS SUPPOSED TO DEAL WITH THE WEIRD SHIT, NOT STUFF WE JUST DON'T HAPPEN TO HAVE AN ANSWER FOR.
SORRY I MISSED YOU WHEN I CAME IN, DETECTIVES...

...BUT THERE'S SOMEONE I'D LIKE YOU TO TALK TO.
DETECTIVE PEZZINI, DETECTIVE GLEASON, THIS IS LUIS ORESTES. HE'S A MAINTENANCE WORKER HERE IN THE BUILDING.
SURE THING, CAPTAIN PEYROUX. BUT UNLESS I'M OVERLOOKING SOMETHING OBVIOUS, I STILL DON'T UNDERSTAND WHY YOU HAD US CALLED INTO THIS.
JUST LISTEN TO WHAT MR. ORESTES HAS TO SAY.
DID YOU SEE WHAT HAPPENED HERE?
I DID.
I WAS WORKING IN THE UPPER STAIRWELL LAST NIGHT, REPAIRING SOME OF THE RAILINGS. THEY GET OLD AND AND THEY GET LOOSE, YOU KNOW?
I HEARD SOMEONE COMING UP THE STAIRS, LIKE THEY WERE RUNNING. IT WAS A MAN, MIDDLE AGED. LOOKED LIKE HE WAS INDIAN.
HE SEEMED WORRIED, OR I GUESS SCARED. I ASKED HIM IF HE NEEDED HELP, BUT HE JUST RAN PAST ME AND KEPT GOING UP THE STAIRS.
I WAS THINKING MAYBE I SHOULD FOLLOW HIM, AND I STARTED TO, BUT THEN I HEARD SOMEONE ELSE RUNNING UP THE STAIRS. BUT FASTER, YOU KNOW?
SO ALMOST BEFORE I COULD TURN AROUND, THIS WOMAN RAN PAST ME. SHE WAS MOVING FAST ENOUGH THAT I COULDN'T BE SURE, BUT I THOUGHT SHE MIGHT'VE BEEN ARMED.
SHE DIDN'T EVEN GIVE ME A SECOND GLANCE, LIKE SHE WASN'T INTERESTED IN ME AT ALL. I WASN'T SURE WHAT I SHOULD DO...
...BUT IT DIDN'T FEEL RIGHT, JUST WALKING AWAY, SO I FOLLOWED THEM ALL THE WAY UP TO THE ROOF.
YOU SHOULD HAVE CALLED THE POLICE IF YOU THOUGHT YOU SAW SOMEONE WHO WAS ARMED.
I REALIZE THAT NOW, BUT I WASN'T THINKING. I JUST FOLLOWED, AND THAT'S WHEN I HEARD THE GUNSHOTS. I PEEKED OUT THE ROOFTOP DOOR AND I SAW...

"...WELL, IT WAS LIKE SOMETHING YOU SEE IN A MOVIE. LIKE A SPACESHIP. THE HATCH WAS OPEN, AND A MAN WAS SHOOTING OUT OF IT, SHOOTING AT THE WOMAN.
"SHE GOT HIT AND WENT DOWN, AND THEN THE FIRST MAN...
"...HE WENT INTO THE SPACESHIP AND THEN THE WHOLE THING JUST DISAPPEARED.
"I DON'T MEAN IT FLEW AWAY, I MEAN IT JUST FADED AWAY."
UM ... OKAY. AND THEN WHAT? WHAT HAPPENED TO THE WOMAN'S BODY?
SEE, THERE WASN'T NO BODY. SHE JUST GOT UP AND WALKED AWAY. WALKED RIGHT PAST ME.
IT'S IMPOSSIBLE, BUT I SAW IT WITH MY OWN EYES.
WHAT CAN YOU TELL US ABOUT THE WOMAN? DESCRIPTION, ANYTHING UNUSUAL ABOUT HER?
"YOU MEAN BESIDES GETTING SHOT BY A DISAPPEARING SPACESHIP AND THEN WALKING AWAY?
"SHE HAD GREEN HAIR, I CAN TELL YOU THAT."
GREEN HAIR?
I GUESS THAT WOULD BE SOMETHING YOU'D REMEMBER.

DETECTIVE GLEASON CAN FINISH TAKING YOUR STATEMENT. I NEED TO GO SPEAK TO MY CAPTAIN.
YEAH, SURE.
YOU GUYS KNOW I'M NOT MAKING THIS UP, RIGHT?
WELL, AT LEAST I KNOW WHY WE'RE HERE NOW.
I GOT WIND OF THIS FROM A FRIEND AT MIDTOWN. I THOUGHT YOU'D WANT TO SNIFF AROUND FOR YOURSELF.
APPRECIATE IT.
YOU KNOW PHIPPS IN INTERNAL AFFAIRS IS STILL LICKING HIS CHOPS TO GET AT YOU.
YOU ACTUALLY PRODUCE THE GREEN-HAIRED PUBLIC MENACE YOU TANGLED WITH A COUPLE MONTHS AGO, PHIPPS MIGHT AS WELL STICK THAT CASE FILE UP HIS OWN ASS.
STAY OUT OF THE WAY OF THE PRESIDING PRECINCT, SHARE ANY EVIDENCE YOU GET. BUT DIG UP WHAT YOU CAN.
UNDERSTOOD, CAPTAIN.
WHAT'VE YOU HEARD FROM THAT DAUGHTER OF YOURS? HOW'S DANI DOING IN NEW ORLEANS?
TALKED TO HER THE OTHER DAY. SOUNDS LIKE SHE'S SETTLING IN.
SHE RENTED THE TOP FLOOR OF AN OLD MANSION HOUSE, AND NOW SHE'S LOOKING FOR A JOB.*
HOPE THIS NEW LIFE WORKS OUT FOR HER.
*READ MORE IN THE ANGELUS TRADE PAPERBACK -FILIP & PHIL

I GOT **NOTHING.** I CALLED IN FAVORS FROM EVERYBODY I COULD THINK OF...

...AND **NOBODY** HAD ANYTHING SOLID. NOT EVEN A SUGGESTION.
ME TOO.
YOUR GREEN-HAIRED **SUPER SOLDIER** GOT SHOT UP BY SOMEBODY THAT DOESN'T EXIST...

...OR AT LEAST BY **AMMO** THAT DOESN'T EXIST.
AND I SERIOUSLY DOUBT **BALLISTICS** IS GOING TO COME THROUGH. A SHOOTING WITH NO APPARENT VICTIM ISN'T TERRIBLY HIGH ON THEIR PRIORITY LIST.

THINK THIS ONE'S A **DEAD END,** SARA.
MAYBE.
BUT I'M NOT **THRILLED** THAT WHOEVER...OR **WHATEVER** SHE IS...IS STILL WALKING AROUND OUT THERE.

NOT **SURPRISED,** EITHER, SINCE SHE
A TANKER TRUCK EXPLODING AS IT WENT INTO THE HUDSON.*
BEST CHANCE OF **FINDING** HER IS TO FIGURE OUT WHO SHOT HER UP ON THAT ROOF.

* WITCHBLADE #119–FILIP & PHIL

Shoot her! Shoot her up!
I THOUGHT YOU WERE GONNA SHOOT **THAT** DAMN THING?
WASTE OF A GOOD BULLET.

CALL IT A NIGHT, COME AT THIS THING FRESH TOMORROW?
SOON.
MY SISTER DOESN'T HAVE PLANS TONIGHT, SO SHE'S COOL WITH LOOKING AFTER HOPE FOR A LITTLE WHILE LONGER.

I'VE GOT TO GET GOING. PROMISED TO TAKE MY DAD OUT TO THE ISLAND SO HE CAN SWAP SHOTS AND STORIES WITH MY UNCLE.
I CAN STOP BY ***LATER,*** IF YOU'LL BE UP.
THAT'D BE NICE.

DON'T STAY TOO LONG.
I WON'T.

I LOVE YOU.
LOVE YOU TOO.

Love you too!
Love you too!
RIGHT, HERE'S A LITTLE TREAT FOR ***YOU.***

Super soldier!

Super soldier!

SUPER SOLDIER...

COME ON, *PICK UP...*

BZZZT
BZZZT
NOT A GOOD TIME...
BZZZT
...REALLY NOT A GOOD TIME.
ARGENT. THIS HAD BETTER BE GOOD, I'M WORKING.
WAIT... WHO IS THIS?
HOW DID YOU EVEN GET THIS NUMBER?
THAT'S RIGHT, I DID, DIDN'T I?
LOOK, DETECTIVE, I'VE GOT AN UNCONSCIOUS, ROGUE ULTRA-SAPIEN AT MY FEET, SO I'M A LITTLE BUSY AT THE MOMENT. YOU WANT TO PLAY TWENTY QUESTIONS, CALL SOMEONE WHO...
WAIT, A GUNSHIP?

A GUNSHIP THAT APPARENTLY DISAPPEARED INTO THIN AIR AFTER SHOOTING UP A GREEN-HAIRED ASSASSIN WHO ALMOST KILLED ME A COUPLE MONTHS AGO...
...AND WHO MAY OR MAY NOT BE SOME KIND OF ROBOT.
THAT'S... NOT SOMETHING I'M FAMILIAR WITH.
BUT A GUNSHIP WITH CLOAKING CAPACITY, THAT'S A LITTLE MORE IN MY WHEELHOUSE.
I'VE GOT A SHELL CASING THAT CAME FROM THE GUNSHIP. LARGE CALIBER, BUT NO MANUFACTURER MARKINGS OF ANY KIND.
CYBERDATA. I'D BET ON IT.
THEY MAKE THEIR OWN HARDWARE TO PREVENT IT BEING TRACED, AND A CLOAKED GUNSHIP IS VERY LAST CENTURY FOR THEM.
GOT ANYTHING ELSE ON CYBERDATA?
TECHNOLOGY CORP SPECIALIZING IN CYBERNETICS. REAL CUTTING-EDGE STUFF A DECADE OR SO AGO.
THEY WENT AWAY WHEN THE DOT-COM BUBBLE BURST. THAT'S THE VERSION FOR PUBLIC CONSUMPTION.
THE TRUTH IS CYBERDATA WAS FOUNDED BY A BUNCH OF EGGHEADS LOOKING TO TAKE OVER THE WORLD.
CAME UP WITH ALL SORTS OF ADVANCED TECH, INCLUDING CYBORGS THEY USED AS COMMANDOS. VERY NASTY.
BUT SOME OF THEIR OWN CREATIONS CAME BACK TO BITE THEM IN THE ASS.
SO ARE THEY STILL OPERATIVE? AND IF THEY ARE...
...WHERE DO I FIND THEM?

YOU KNOW THAT COCKROACH YOU THINK YOU SQUASHED INTO PASTE, BUT IT ALWAYS COMES BACK? THAT'S CYBERDATA.
THEY WENT UNDERGROUND FOR A WHILE, BUT NOW THEY'RE BACK IN A MAJOR WAY WITH THOSE JETT SMARTPHONES.
MOST OF THEIR FACILITIES STILL APPEAR TO BE EMPTY, BUT WITH SOME OF THEM, IT'S JUST WINDOW DRESSING.
ASSUMING THAT WAS A CYBERDATA GUNSHIP, THE CLOSEST SITE TO YOU WOULD BE IN WESTCHESTER, AN ABANDONED MANUFACTURING PLANT NORTH OF YONKERS.
I OWE YOU, ARGENT. THANKS.
SINCE YOU SEEM TO BE IN A CHATTY MOOD, HOW 'BOUT TELLING ME WHO YOU REALLY WORK FOR?
YOU FIRST. WHY DON'T YOU FILL ME IN ON THAT PRETTY LITTLE BRACELET YOU HAVE?
GOODBYE, PEZZINI.
DEET
GLEASON
NO.
SHOULDN'T BOTHER HIM FOR A WILD GOOSE CHASE.

ALL RIGHT...
...SO I'M NOT THE ONLY ONE HERE.

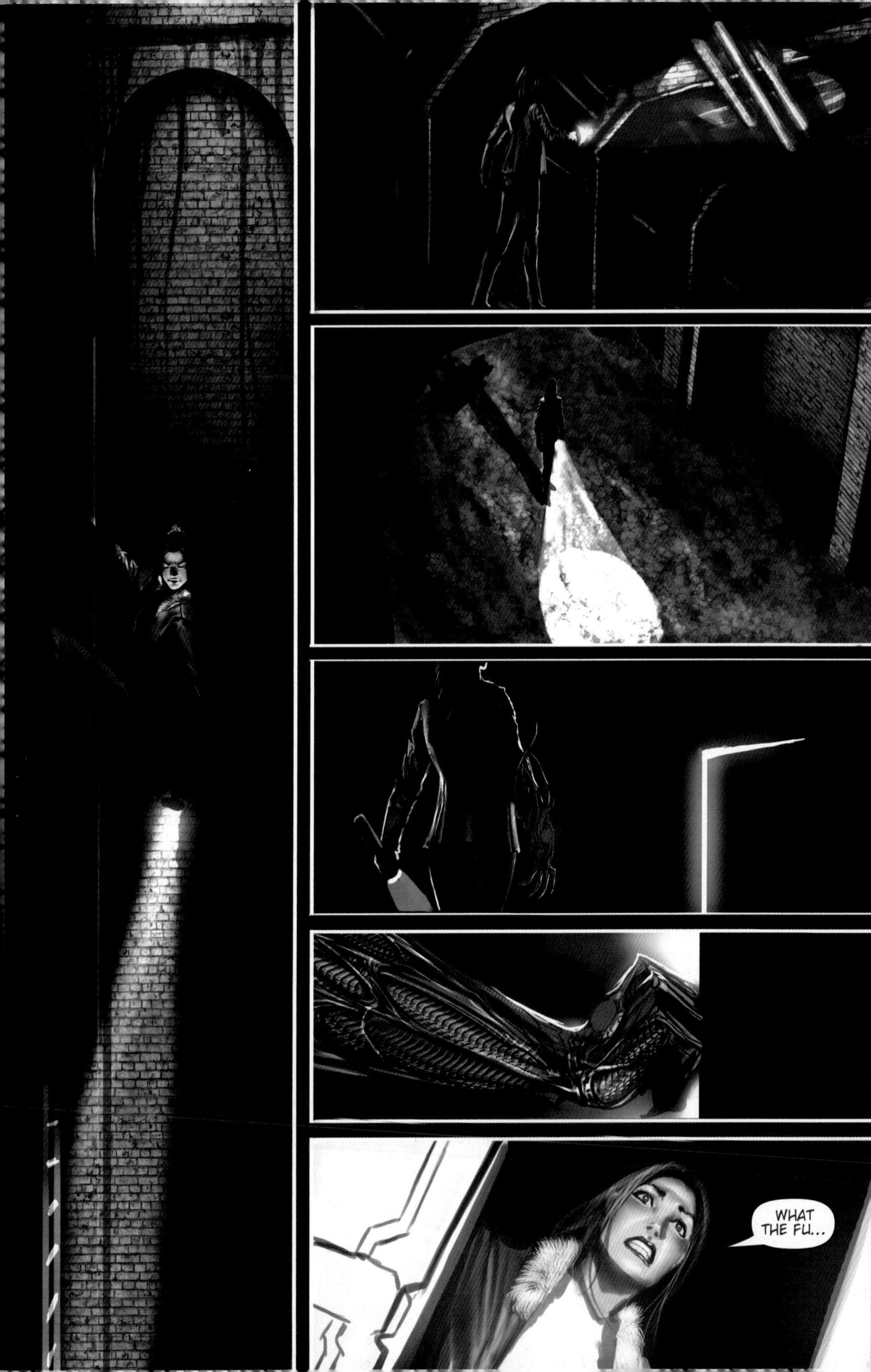
WHAT THE FU...

...GHHH?!

YOU SHOULD NOT HAVE ***FOLLOWED*** ME.

LADY, I STILL DON'T EVEN KNOW WHO THE HELL YOU ARE...
...BUT THIS TIME I'M DAMN SURE GONNA FIND OUT.
YOU'RE NOT MY TARGET...
...BUT I WON'T LET YOU KEEP ME FROM MY TARGET.
LET ME GUESS...
...NO PERMIT, RIGHT?
INTRUDERS...

...YOU ARE TRESPASSING ON CYBERDATA PROPERTY.
ALL TRESPASSERS ARE TO BE EXECUTED.

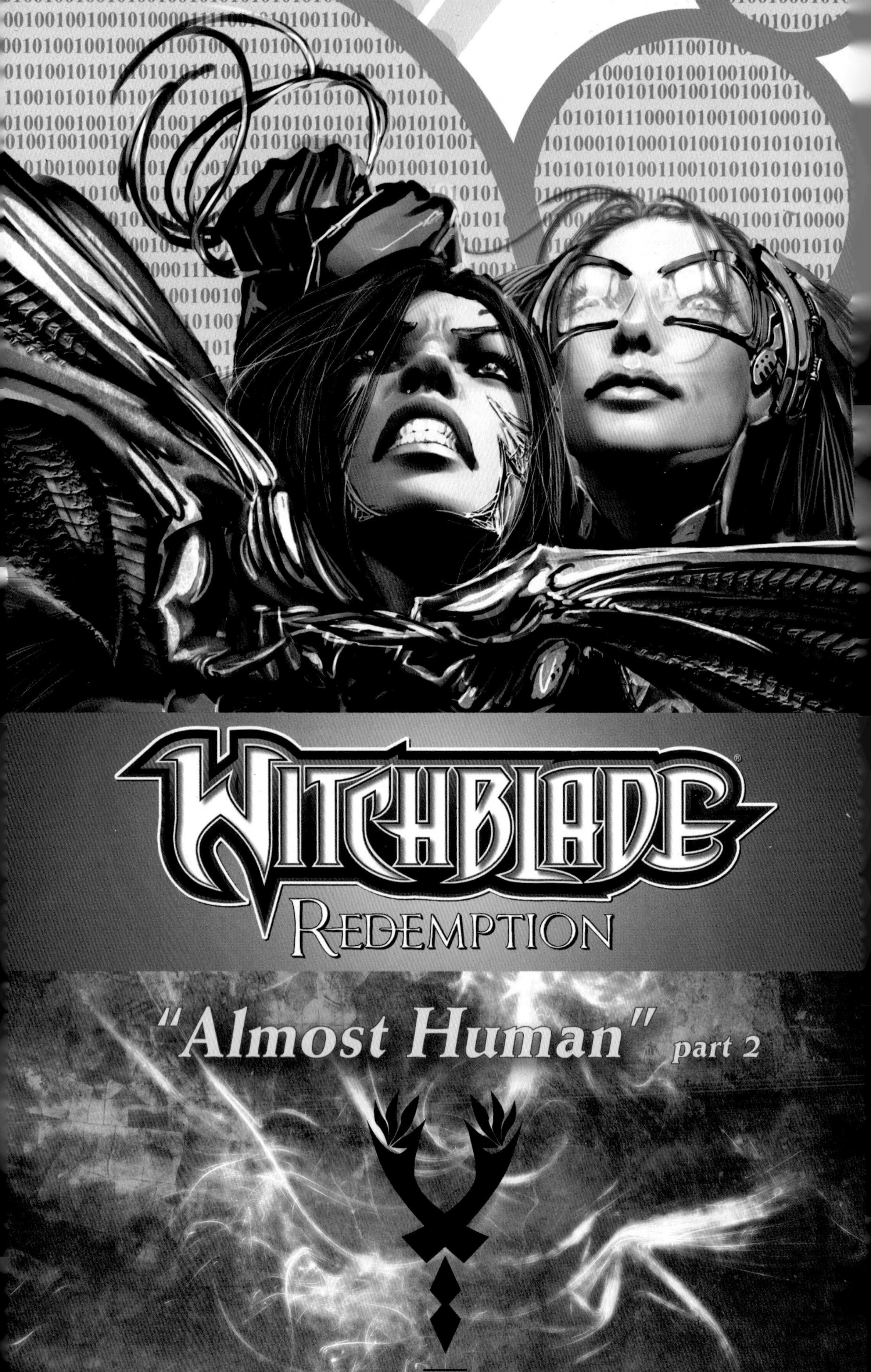
WITCHBLADE®
REDEMPTION
"Almost Human" part 2

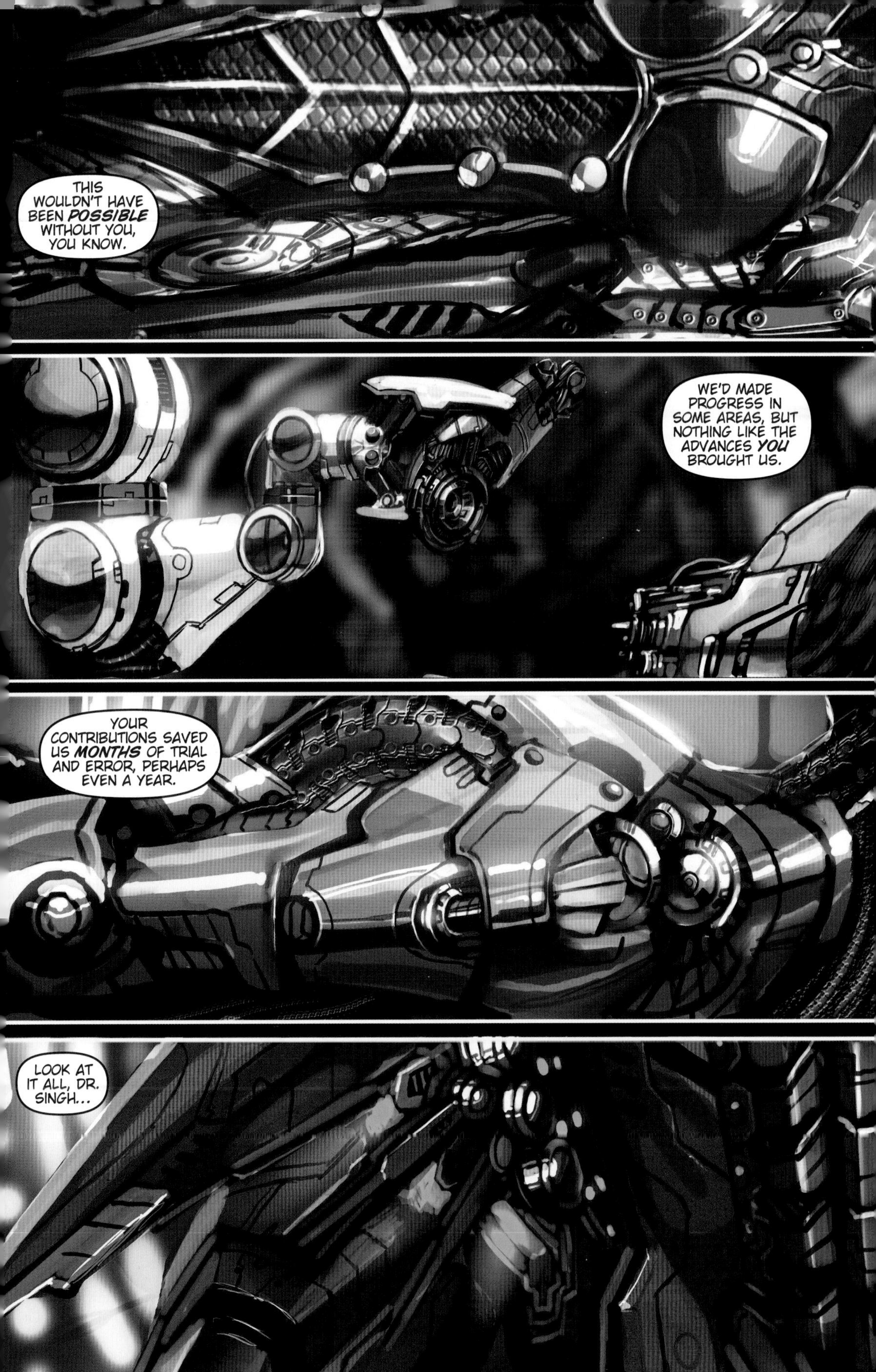
THIS WOULDN'T HAVE BEEN *POSSIBLE* WITHOUT YOU, YOU KNOW.
WE'D MADE PROGRESS IN SOME AREAS, BUT NOTHING LIKE THE ADVANCES *YOU* BROUGHT US.
YOUR CONTRIBUTIONS SAVED US *MONTHS* OF TRIAL AND ERROR, PERHAPS EVEN A YEAR.
LOOK AT IT ALL, DR. SINGH...

...*THIS* IS WHAT YOU'VE WROUGHT.
WE'VE ADDED SOME MODIFICATIONS OF OUR OWN, OF COURSE, BUT *NONE* OF THIS WOULD BE HERE WITHOUT WHAT YOU BROUGHT US.

CYBERDATA IS GRATEFUL.
YOU *SHOULD* BE...

...I DELIVERED WHAT YOU WANTED AT CONSIDERABLE PERSONAL RISK.
AND YOU RECEIVED CONSIDERABLE PERSONAL *REWARD,* DOCTOR.

I'M JUST GLAD YOU WERE MORE PRAGMATIC THAN YOUR FELLOW RESEARCHERS.
THEY BELIEVED THE PROGRAM WOULD EVENTUALLY MAKE THEM WEALTHY BEYOND ALL DREAMS OF AVARICE. BUT I WAS TIRED OF WAITING.
WHAT'S THIS? WHAT'S GOING ON?
SECURITY ALERT.
THERE'S BEEN A FACILITY BREACH, DOCTORS. WE EXPECT TO HAVE THE MATTER RESOLVED SHORTLY...
...BUT WE'LL MOVE YOU TO A SECURE LOCATION AS A PRECAUTION.
WHAT DO YOU MEAN A BREACH? IT'S HER, ISN'T IT?!
SHE'S HERE AND YOU'RE NOT TELLING ME!
YOU NEED NOT BE CONCERNED, DR. SINGH. THE INCIDENT IS AT THE FAR END OF THE COMPLEX.
CYBERDATA WILL KEEP YOU SAFE.

...YOU ARE TRESPASSING ON *CYBERDATA PROPERTY*.
ALL TRESPASSERS ARE TO BE *EXECUTED*.

FRIENDS OF YOURS?

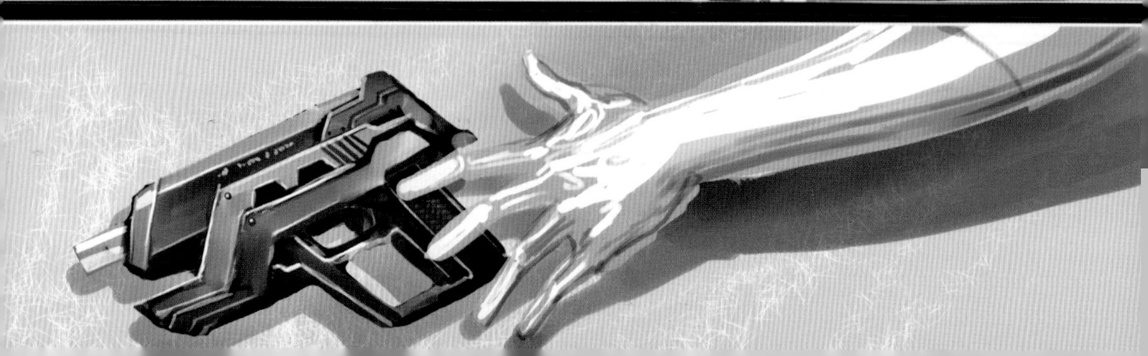

PHOOM
PHOOM

OKAY, SO I GUESS *TALKING* ABOUT IT IS OUT OF THE QUESTION...

THESE THINGS ARE JUST WALKING *TIN CANS...*
PHOOM
SHINNK

...WHO'S *RUNNING* THEM?
SHRAAAK

PHOOM PHOOM
SHUNNK
NEXT-GENERATION BRAIN BOXES IMPRINTED WITH USER ENGRAMS.
WHATEVER THAT MEANS.
S.H.O.C. SQUAD ONE REQUESTING REINFORCEMENTS. WE NEED--
PHOOM

AS LONG AS I'M NOT TAKING OUT *PEOPLE*...

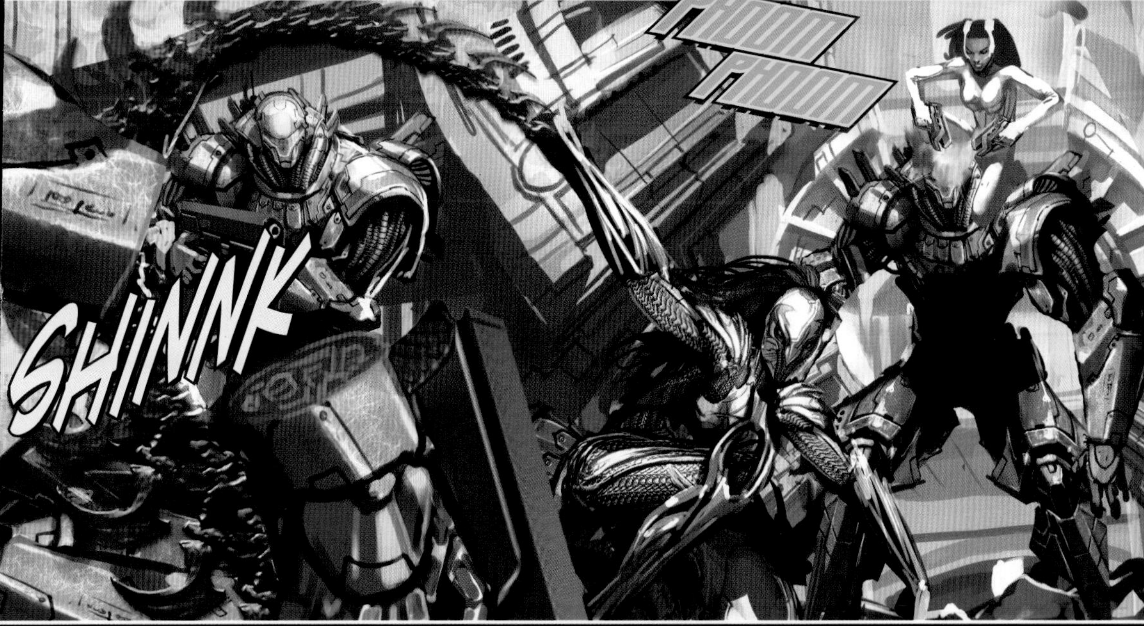

...NNNHH...

IF YOU'RE GONNA PULL A TRIGGER...

CHOOM
...DO IT BEFORE SOMEBODY BEATS YOU TO IT.

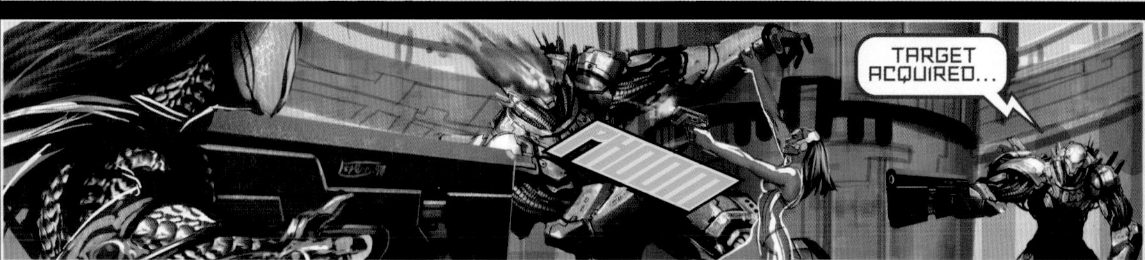
CHOOM
TARGET ACQUIRED...

HN?
CHOOM

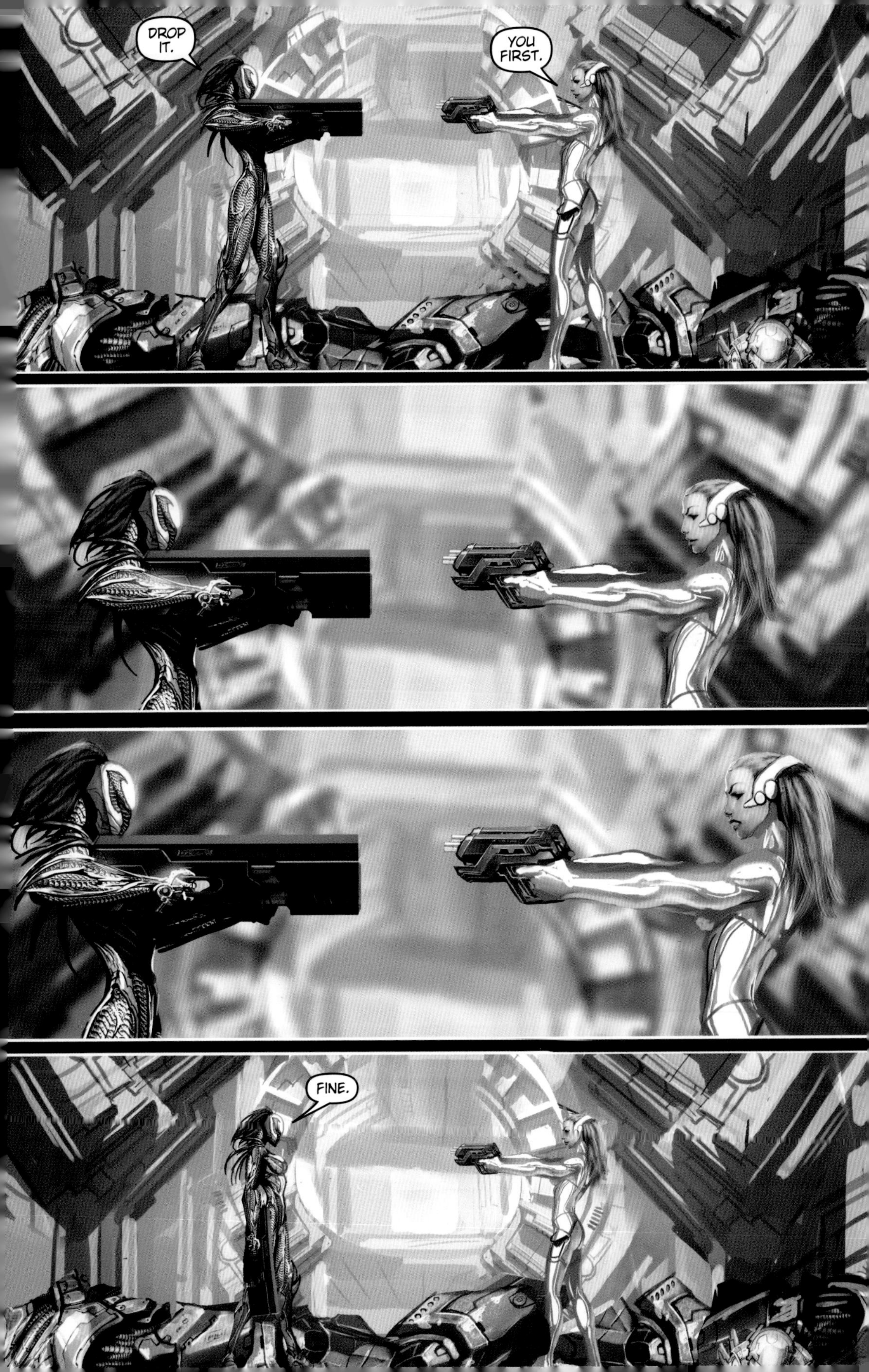
DROP IT.
YOU FIRST.
FINE.

IF WE WERE GOING TO SHOOT EACH OTHER, WE COULD'VE DONE IT BEFORE THIS. BUT DO ME A FAVOR...
...TELL ME WHO YOU ARE.
I SAVED YOU FROM GETTING YOUR HEAD BLOWN OFF, SO IT'S THE LEAST YOU CAN DO AFTER TRYING TO KILL ME.
TWICE.
I AM CALLED APHRODITE IV.
WHAT, YOU MEAN LIKE APHRODITE FOR PRESIDENT?
THERE WERE THREE OTHER MODELS BEFORE ME. I AM THE FOURTH.
SOUNDS MORE LIKE YOUR PORN NAME. BUT YOU DON'T STRIKE ME AS A STRIPPER WORKING YOUR WAY THROUGH COLLEGE.
SO WHO THE HELL ARE YOU?
IT IS MORE A QUESTION OF WHAT I AM.

I AM A CYBORG, THE FOURTH SUCH VERSION SINCE THE IMPLEMENTATION OF THE PROGRAM.
I WAS DESIGNED AND BUILT BY A PRIVATE CONSORTIUM OF SCIENTISTS SPECIALIZING IN ARTIFICIAL INTELLIGENCE.
MY PRIMARY FUNCTION IS TO OBEY MY OPERATING PARAMETERS AND MISSION-SPECIFIC INITIATIVES, BUT I AM ABLE TO MAKE COGNITIVE DECISIONS AS WELL.
THOUGH I AM CAPABLE OF PERFORMING A WIDE RANGE OF FUNCTIONS, MY PRINCIPAL USE IS INTENDED TO BE AS A COMBAT AND ESPIONAGE UNIT.
EVENTUALLY, I AM TO BE REPLICATED SO THAT THERE WILL BE MANY VERSIONS OF ME TO BE SOLD TO THE HIGHEST BIDDERS.
I AM A WEAPON.
MY FIRST ASSIGNMENT WAS YOU, DETECTIVE SARA PEZZINI, NEW YORK POLICE DEPARTMENT SHIELD NUMBER 1011...
...IN ORDER THAT MY CAPABILITIES COULD BE TESTED AGAINST AN OPPONENT OF SUPERIOR ABILITY.
CHAK

HOW DID YOU KNOW ALL THAT? ABOUT ME, I MEAN.
YOU ARE KNOWN TO THOSE WHO CREATED ME, JUST AS JACKIE ESTACADO WAS KNOWN TO THEM.

DON'T LIKE THAT AT ALL.
SO WHY ARE YOU BREAKING INTO A SECRET CYBERDATA FACILITY?

I AM TO ASSASSINATE DR. ASHISH SINGH, A FORMER MEMBER OF THE CONSORTIUM THAT CREATED ME.
DR. SINGH STOLE MY MODEL'S DESIGNS IN ORDER TO SELL THEM. DR. SINGH IS HERE.

WAIT... WHAT?

YOU THINK I'M GOING TO LET YOU WALK AWAY AND DO THAT?

REMAIN WHERE YOU ARE!
SHIT...

...MORE COMPANY.
YOU ARE TRESPASSING ON CYBERDATA PROPERTY.
ALL TRESPASSERS ARE TO BE EXECUTED.
YEAH, YEAH...
...HEARD IT ALL BEFORE.
PHOOM
PHOOM

BREEP
BREEP

BREEP
BREEP

HEY, I'M ON THE MAJOR DEEGAN, BRINGING MY DAD BACK HOME NOW. HE AND MY UNCLE TIED ONE ON.
IT'LL BE ON THE *LATE* SIDE WHEN I'VE GOT HIM SETTLED, BUT I CAN STILL SWING BY IF YOU WANT.

GLEASON, SORRY, IT'S NOT SARA, IT'S *JULIE.*
I'M ACTUALLY *LOOKING* FOR SARA. SHE HASN'T GOTTEN HOME YET. I TRIED HER CELL, BUT SHE DIDN'T PICK UP.
HWAAAH!

SHE HASN'T? SHE'S NOT WITH ME, I LEFT HER AT THE OFFICE HOURS AGO. YOU TRIED THE OFFICE LINE?
NO, SHE SAID SHE WAS GOING TO WORK A LITTLE LONGER, THEN HEAD HOME.
I WOULD'VE STAYED WITH HER, BUT I PROMISED MY DAD I'D DRIVE HIM OUT TO THE ISLAND.
HE'S CURRENTLY DREAMING OF THE OLD COUNTRY, WITH A SNOOT FULL OF JAMESON'S.
I LEFT VOICEMAILS AND TEXTED HER. NOTHING. HOPE IS GETTING PRETTY FUSSY, SHE WON'T GO TO SLEEP.
SHE WANTS HER MOM.
MAMA... MAMA...
I NEED TO DROP OFF MY DAD, BUT THEN I'LL TRACK HER DOWN, OKAY?
THANKS, GLEASON. THAT WOULD BE GREAT.
I'M SURE I'M JUST OVER-REACTING, BUT AFTER EVERYTHING WHEN SARA WAS... NOT HERSELF... I JUST WANT TO BE SURE.
CAN'T HURT TO CHECK, BUT I'M POSITIVE SHE'S FINE.
IF THERE'S ONE THING WE BOTH KNOW ABOUT YOUR SISTER...

"...IT'S THAT SHE CAN TAKE CARE OF HERSELF."
KLUNK
APHRODITE, WAIT.
WHERE DO YOU THINK YOU'RE GOING?
I SAID STOP.
I'M NOT LETTING YOU JUST STALK A MAN AND EXECUTE HIM.
IT DOES NOT CONCERN YOU.
IT DAMN WELL DOES CONCERN ME!
I'M A COP!

I DON'T CARE IF YOU ARE JUST R2-D2 WITH NICE TITS, YOU DON'T GET TO MURDER SOMEONE. ESPECIALLY ON MY WATCH.
HAVEN'T YOU KILLED PEOPLE?
I HAVE.
BUT IT WAS IN THE LINE OF DUTY, WHEN THERE WAS NO OTHER CHOICE.
HOW IS THAT DIFFERENT? THIS IS MY DUTY.
TAKING A LIFE IS... EASY.
NOT THAT LONG AGO I GOT A LOOK AT WHAT I'D BE LIKE IF I WENT DOWN THAT PATH. I DIDN'T LIKE WHAT I SAW.
JUST BECAUSE YOU'RE NOT HUMAN DOESN'T MEAN YOU DON'T NEED SOME BIT OF HUMANITY.

YOU SAID THIS MAN STOLE FROM YOUR...EMPLOYERS? CREATORS? WHATEVER YOU'D CALL THEM. THAT'S A CRIME. I CAN ARREST HIM FOR IT.
HE'LL BE PUNISHED, BUT NOT IN THE WAY YOU INTENDED.

LET ME DO THAT, INSTEAD OF WHAT YOU HAVE IN MIND.
VERY WELL.

YOUR WAY.

SO WHEN WE FIND YOUR DR. SINGH, I ARREST HIM, RIGHT? DON'T GET TRIGGER HAPPY.
ANY IDEA WHERE HE'D BE?
SOMEWHERE NEAR HERE. IF THE SCHEMATICS I DOWNLOADED ARE STILL VALID, THIS SHOULD BE THE RESEARCH LABORATORY.
NO GUARDS? LITTLE CURIOUS, DON'T YOU THINK?
DOESN'T MATTER.
EASY THERE, ANNIE OAKLEY.
HOW 'BOUT WE DO IT THE QUIET WAY?

SO, APHRODITE...

...WHY DIDN'T YOU TELL ME YOU HAD FAMILY?

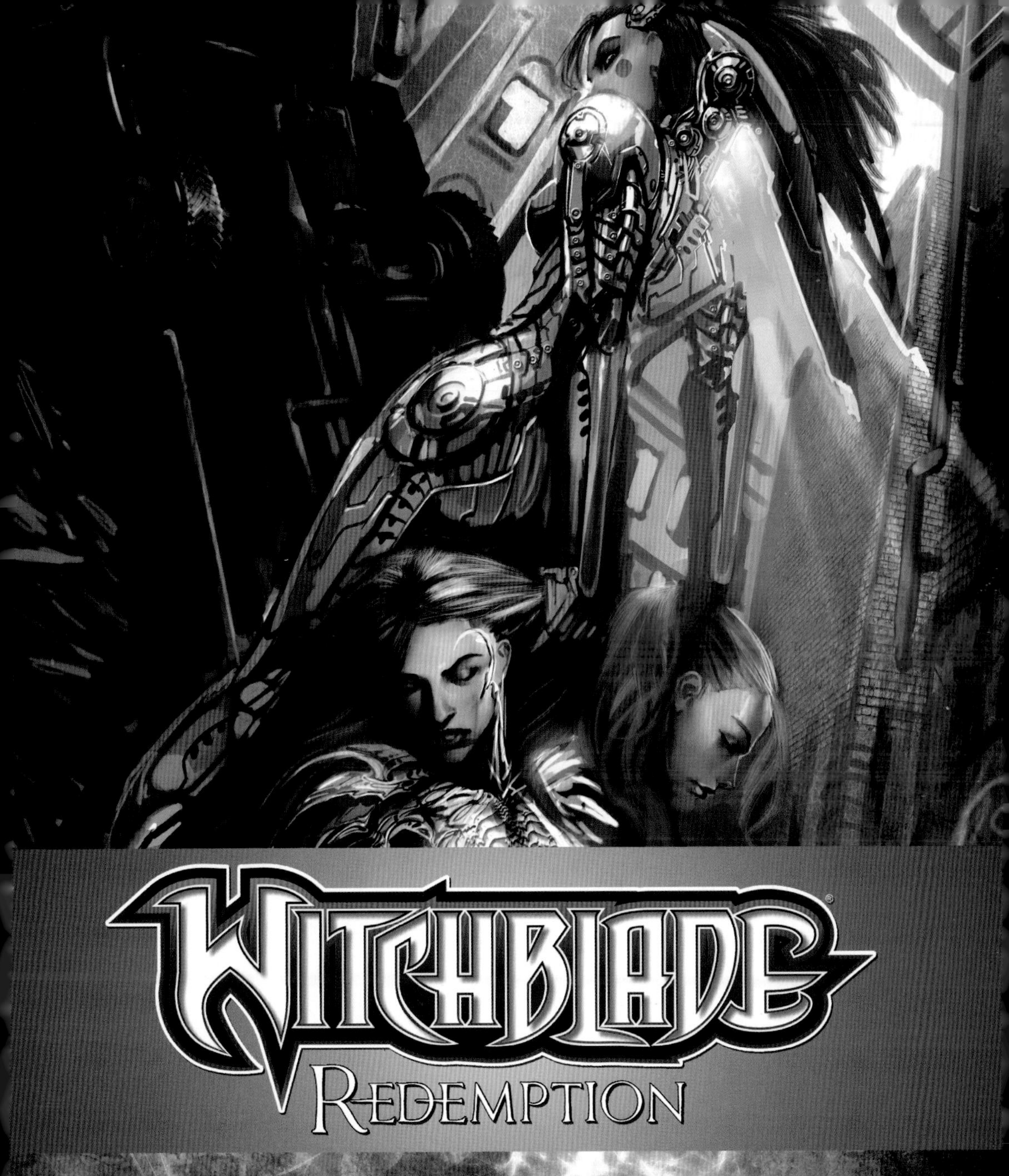

WITCHBLADE® REDEMPTION

"Almost Human" part 3

I TOLD YOU, IT IS HER! IT'S APHRODITE! I DON'T KNOW WHO THE OTHER ONE IS...

...BUT LOOK AT THEM. THE DOORS WERE NOTHING TO THEM, THEY JUST WALKED RIGHT INTO THE LAB AS IF...

...NO.
NO, NO, NO.
YOU SEE? SHE KNOWS WE'RE WATCHING...

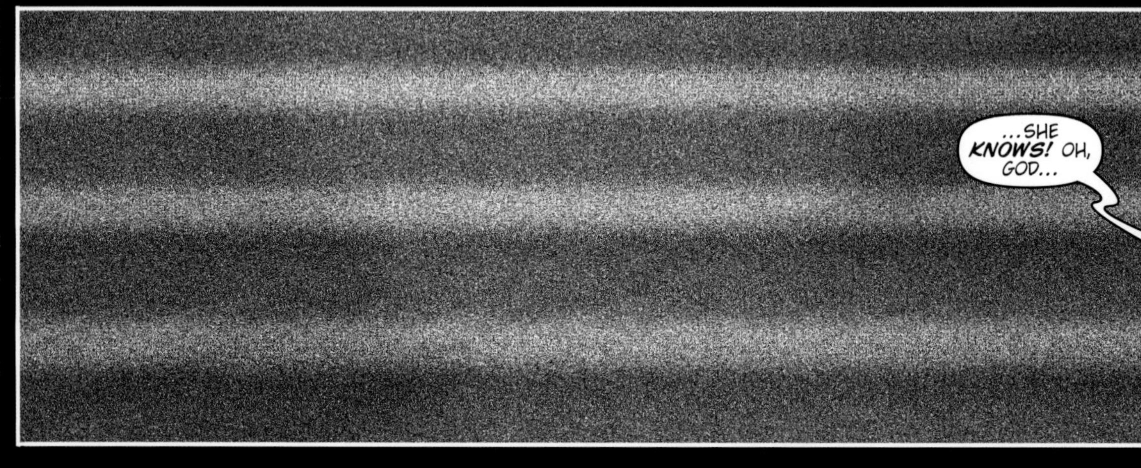
...SHE KNOWS! OH, GOD...

...SHE'LL COME AND FIND ME!

CYBERDATA WILL INSURE YOUR SAFETY, DR. SINGH.

PLEASE FOLLOW ME SO I CAN DELIVER YOU BOTH TO A SECURE LOCATION.

THE ONLY ***SECURE LOCATION*** IS FAR AWAY FROM HERE! YOU DON'T UNDERSTAND WHAT SHE ***IS!***

THERE ARE MORE LIKE YOU?
THERE DIDN'T USED TO BE.
THEN I'VE GOT NEWS FOR YOU APHRODITE. YOU'RE NOT AN ONLY CHILD ANYMORE.

I WAS A UNIQUE CREATION BY MY DESIGNERS.
THESE MUST HAVE BEEN CREATED HERE, BY CYBERDATA.
PWHH!

BUT THESE THINGS ARE LIKE YOU.
SINGH SOLD MY DESIGN SPECIFICATIONS TO CYBERDATA.
THESE MODELS ARE EXTRAPOLATIONS ON MY DESIGN. THEY'VE BEEN GIVEN SPECIFIC AUGMENTATIONS LIKE SPEED...
...INCREASED COMBAT SKILLS...
...OR FLIGHT.
SO LIKE YOU...
...BUT EVEN WORSE.
CHANK

UNGH!
LIKE HER...
...BUT EVEN BETTER.
PHOOM PHOOM
WE'LL SEE ABOUT BETTER.
HERA! I NEED YOU!
BUSY.
ARTEMIS, HELP YOUR SISTER.
KRANG

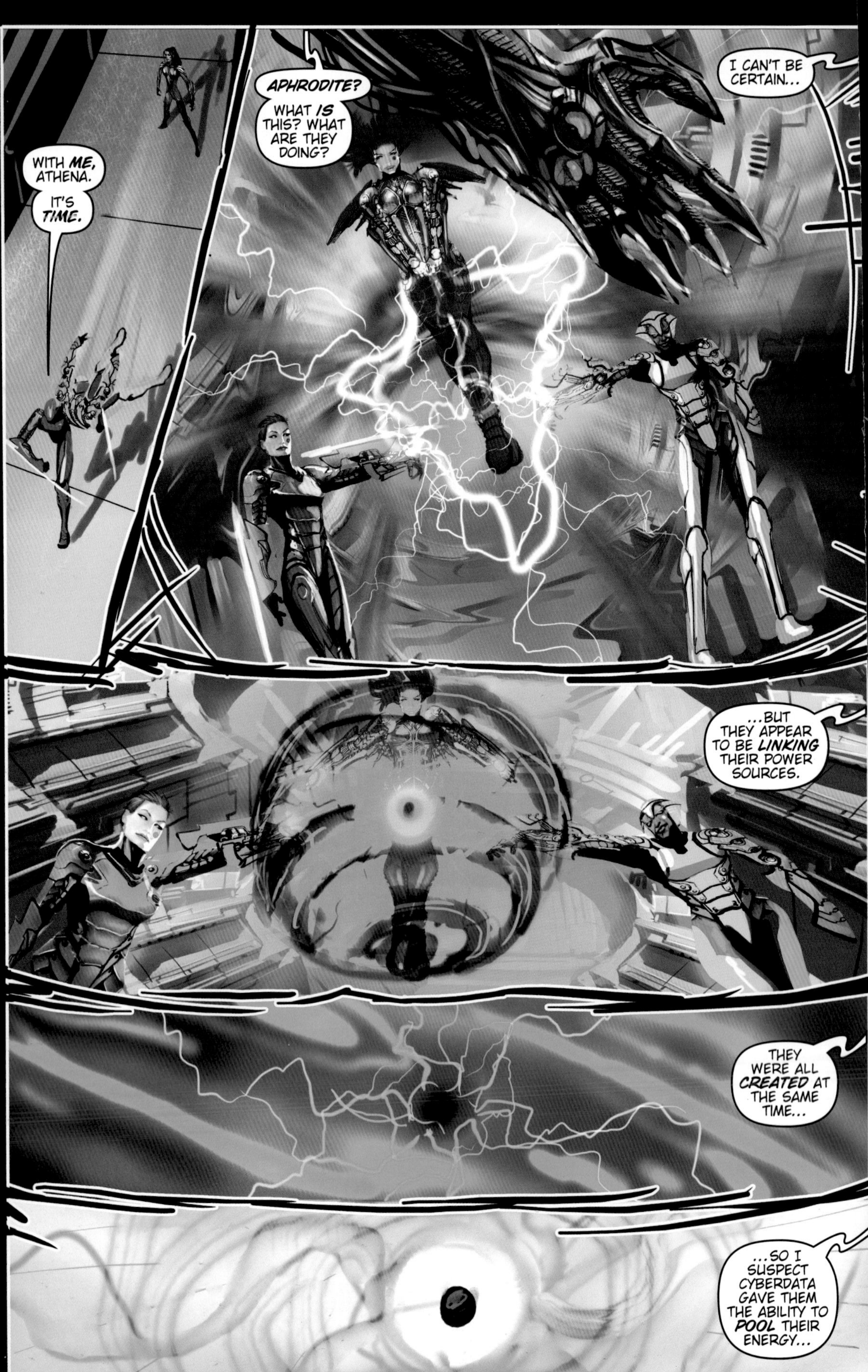

WITH ME, ATHENA.
IT'S TIME.
APHRODITE? WHAT IS THIS? WHAT ARE THEY DOING?
I CAN'T BE CERTAIN...
...BUT THEY APPEAR TO BE LINKING THEIR POWER SOURCES.
THEY WERE ALL CREATED AT THE SAME TIME...
...SO I SUSPECT CYBERDATA GAVE THEM THE ABILITY TO POOL THEIR ENERGY...

...AND PROJECT IT.
KINDA MAKES YOU LOOK LIKE LAST YEAR'S MODEL.
BUT YOU KNOW WHAT?
I'VE HAD MY FILL OF ALL THIS CYBORG SHIT...

...AND I'VE GOT MY OWN UPGRADE.
GHLLG

HRRK?
KRACHANK

PLEASE, SISTER...
...YOU COULD JOIN US.
WE ARE YOU.
NOT ANYMORE.
PHOOM
YOU THINK YOUR DR. SINGH IS STILL IN THIS FACILITY SOMEWHERE?
HE'LL BE HERE.
THEN REMEMBER OUR AGREEMENT. MY WAY, NOT YOURS.
I'LL ARREST HIM.
I REMEMBER.

WHAT MAKES YOU BELIEVE SINGH IS STILL HERE? IF HE'S SO VALUABLE, WHY WOULDN'T CYBERDATA MOVE HIM?
BECAUSE THEY NEVER EXPECTED ME TO SHOW UP. OR YOU.
AND EVEN IF THEY DID, THEY'RE ARROGANT ENOUGH TO THINK WE'RE NOT A SERIOUS THREAT.
ALL RIGHT, ASSUMING WE FIND SINGH AND I ARREST HIM...WHAT HAPPENS NEXT? FOR YOU, I MEAN?
WHERE DO YOU GO FROM HERE?
BACK TO MY CREATORS.
SO THEY CAN KEEP USING YOU? DON'T YOU WANT TO BE MORE THAN JUST A SERVANT?
I KNOW SOMEONE WHO MIGHT BE ABLE TO HELP YOU. SHE'S USED TO DEALING WITH PEOPLE WHO ARE...OUT OF THE ORDINARY. IN FACT, SHE'S THE ONE WHO--
APHRODITE?
PHOOM
AHHNN!

I WON'T ALLOW YOU TO COMPROMISE MY MISSION.
...YOU SAID...
...YOU AGREED WE'D DO THIS... MY WAY...
I LIED.
SHUNK!
THEN I GUESS YOU ARE LEARNING TO BE HUMAN...
AHHG!

GHH!
HNNNNN...

HHNN?
NEVER SHOULD'VE TRUSTED THE BITCH.
SHIT.

SHIT.
SARA?

SARA!
CRISSAKES, I DIDN'T KNOW IF I WAS GONNA FIND YOU IN ONE PIECE OR NOT. ARE YOU OKAY?
BETTER THAN THE PEOPLE ON THE OTHER SIDE OF THIS DOOR.

I'M FINE, GLEASON. WHAT'RE YOU EVEN DOING HERE?
I TRACKED YOUR CAR'S TRANSCEIVER, BUT THIS ISN'T QUITE WHAT I EXPECTED. WHAT ***IS*** THIS PLACE?

AND WHY DIDN'T YOU ***CALL*** ME?
I GOT A LITTLE... BUSY.
SORRY.

IS THIS ABOUT THE ***GREEN-HAIRED*** WOMAN? IS ***SHE*** RESPONSIBLE FOR ALL THIS?
CONNECT THE DOTS FOR ME, SARA.
TURNS OUT SHE WASN'T A ***WOMAN*** AT ALL.

LOOK, I CAN FILL IN ALL THE DETAILS LATER. SHORT VERSION, SHE'S A CYBORG, WHICH IS NOT EVEN CLOSE TO THE MOST OUTLANDISH THING I'VE EVER SAID TO YOU.

SHE WAS TRACKING ONE OF THE SCIENTISTS WHO CREATED HER. HE'S CURRENTLY IN THERE WITH HIS BRAINS SPLATTERED ACROSS THE WALL.

I'M SURE APHRODITE--THAT'S HER NAME--IS LONG GONE BY NOW.

SO NOT THE ***BEST*** NIGHT I'VE EVER HAD, IN CASE YOU WERE WONDERING.

KILLER ROBOTS ARE A LITTLE ABOVE MY PAY GRADE. BUT YOU STILL COULD'VE LET ME KNOW.
IF WE'RE GOING TO BE PARTNERS--AS DETECTIVES AND OTHERWISE--YOU HAVE TO INCLUDE ME, SARA.
YOU'RE RIGHT. I SAID I WAS SORRY, AND I AM.
I THOUGHT I HAD THE SITUATION UNDER CONTROL. I THOUGHT I HAD HER CONVINCED THAT NO ONE NEEDED TO DIE.
BUT SHE PLAYED ME.
SO WHAT DO WE DO ABOUT ALL THIS? I'M NOT SURE CRIME SCENE WOULD QUITE KNOW WHERE TO BEGIN.
SEAL IT UP AND WALK AWAY.
THIS PLACE IS MOSTLY TRASHED FROM THE BATTLE ANYWAY, AND I CAN TAKE APART ANYTHING THAT ISN'T.
APHRODITE LOOKS LIKE US, BUT THERE'S NOTHING HUMAN ABOUT HER. SHE DOESN'T FEEL ANYTHING.
I MADE THE MISTAKE OF SHOWING HER SOME SYMPATHY. BUT I'D RATHER DO THAT...
...THAN EVER BECOME LIKE HER.
I JUST WANT TO GO HOME AND SEE MY LITTLE GIRL.

DR. PALMER?
DR. VOLCKERT?
DR. YEBOAH?
IS ANYONE HERE?
ANYONE?

Witchblade®
Redemption
Cover Gallery

Witchblade, issue #131 Cover A
art by: **Stjepan Sejic**

Witchblade, issue #131 Cover B
art by: **Chris Bachalo** and **Tim Townsend**

Witchblade, issue #131 Cover C
art by: **John Tyler Christopher**

Witchblade, issue #131 Cover D "All Beef Edition"
art by: **John Tyler Christopher**

Witchblade, issue #131 Cover E, Baltimore Comic Con variant
art by: **Stjepan Sejic**

Witchblade, issue #131 Cover F, Baltimore Comic Con Fantastic Realm variant
art by: **Ale Garza** and **Nei Ruffino**

Witchblade, issue #131 Cover G, Albany Comic Con variant
art by: **Matthew Dow Smith** and **Charlie Kirchoff**

Witchblade, issue #132 Cover A
art by: **Stjepan Sejic**

NB2
RAWINN

Witchblade, issue #132 Cover B
art by: **Nelson Blake II, Ryan Winn** and **Arif Prianto** of IFS

Witchblade, issue #132 Cover C, Virginia Comic-Con variant
art by: **Randy Green** and **Felix Serrano**

Witchblade, issue #132 Cover D. Virginia Comic-Con Virgin variant
art by: **Randy Green**

Witchblade, issue #133 Cover A
art by: Stjepan Sejic

Witchblade, issue #133 Cover B
art by: **Jeffrey Spokes**

Witchblade, issue #134 Cover B
art by: **Michal Ivan**

Witchblade, issue #135 Cover A
art by: **Stjepan Sejic**

Witchblade, issue #135 Cover B
art by: **Darick Robertson** and **JD Smith**

Witchblade, issue #136 Cover A
art by: **Stjepan Sejic**

Witchblade, issue #136 Cover B, Washington Comic-Con variant
art by: **JG Jones** and **Dave McCaig**

Witchblade, issue #136 Cover C, Washington Comic-Con Virgin variant
art by: JG Jones
LIEUTENANT
1101
JG JONES

Cover Process Gallery

Take an inside look at the evolution of the covers from this collection, in the words of the artists, editors and writer.

John Tyler Christopher

issue #131 Cover C process

Gents

Attached are 3 concepts for the Witchblade 131 cover. I narrowed it down to these; but I have additional ideas on the same theme, so please let me know if you like to see more. The first 2 are pretty straight-forward, but the 3rd is pretty intense (so please bear with me).

1. Sara literally coming out of the "wall of witchblade". Her legs are still enveloped, but you can see where her hands are setting just inside the mass. Her hair is billowing behind her as a framing devise for her upper body form.

2. I sent this to you guys as a sketch for 129. The hand still needs moved down so that it is completely framed by the hair.

3. I checked out some of the forums online, and it seems people are getting the yin-yang aspect of 129, so I wanted to give an option that keeps the visual commentary angle going.

This idea is a different take on using negative space. The concept is very metaphor heavy, commenting on the conclusion of the War of the Witchblades, and the price of conflict resolution and the return to balance. Obviously I haven't read the final chapter of the arc, but I believe the idea of the cover is broad enough tha speaks to the difficulty at the end of any battle, and the balancing concept of the Witchblade only plays it out even more poignant.

The cover is half black and half white. Sara is standing in the middle. Her skin is painted in full color, while her armor is a 50% grey. The light is coming down from above, and allowing the highlights on the armor to blend into the white side, while the shadows blend into the black side. The blending of the 2 sides into armor is similar to the Scarface poster I've attached. Except the 50% grey included into the armor palette.

Her hands are out to her side holding plates. Her hair is set up as a framing device, but also to allude to a scale. On the black side there is a white dove, in mid flight, picking up an olive branch from the plate, and on the white side there is a black crow picking at a plate with a pound of flesh. Sara's expression is subtle, with a grin and a tear.

After all that, it's probably important to mention that Sara would still be crazy hot!

Let me know what you think.

Thanks
John

Filip and Phil

Good morning. Attached is a sketch of the 131 cover. I repositioned her a bit to make her pose more dynamic. I'm also still playing with her head and expression.

With the background being filled with detail, I plan on separating the parts of the armor that are out of the wall with a black stroke, while the rest of the background and detail will be a very dark grey. I hope this will insinuate shape while still forcing it to be viewed as negative space.

Please let me know what you think.

Thanks
John

Guys

Attached is a revised sketch for the 131 cover. I wanted to get you something before Friday so I can really hit it hard this weekend.

I fixed a lot of the anatomical issues and I repositioned her head.

Please let me know what you think.

Thanks
John

Gentlemen

I wanted to give you a status report on the 131 cover. Attached you will find a work in progress.

The attached file might scare you into thinking I've abandoned the negative space idea, but I assure you the final piece will have a feel very reminiscent to the White Queen piece in my portfolio, while still adding elements exclusive to our favorite gauntlet wearing cop.

I decided to take a page from the book of Sook (Ryan that is) and create the negative space of the armor and background using a color hold on detailed inks. Although at this stage the armor appears to be positive, I'm going to give it a color hold of roughly 15-20% grey/blue, while the background will be set at around the 10% mark. This will make the negative space have elements of interest and still be used to frame the fully painted flesh and hair. It will also allow this space to have the feel of metal, without utilizing harsh values. The segmented under-armor and gems will be created using color holds, but with an intensity between the skin and armor. Parts will have black outlines, similar to the White Queen, to define the graphic meta-shapes

I plan on completing this cover next week, please let me know if you need it before then.

Thanks
John

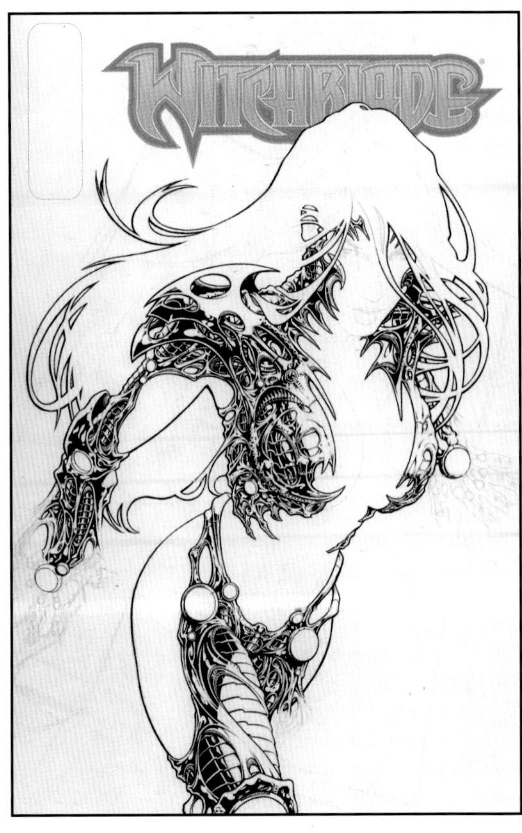

left, variant cover concept

right, final cover

Stjepan Sejic
issue #132 Cover A process

Hey Stjepan,

I think we want to keep away from showing much of the troll on the cover, since that's a big reveal at the end of the issue. So:

1) A shot of Sara in her armor on the wooden bridge that figures in the story; the troll's arm is coming up from under the bridge, grabbing a surprised Sara by the ankle.

2) Sexy, alluring shot of Sara in bed, sheet pulled up to cover her breasts, looking right at the reader. Her right hand is extended toward the reader, gauntlet on the hand, making a "come closer" gesture with her forefinger.

3) More of a pin-up image of Sara in the woods, some spooky trees around her. Sara is framed by a huge full moon that's rising at the horizon line.

-Filip, Ron & Phil

right, troll design

right, final cover

Nelson Blake II

issue #132 Cover B process

I figured out my themes...unless you object of course. The first and most important step for me was to dissect the themes of Witchblade that we'd use to springboard the imagery from. Feel free to chime in on this, but I see the Witchblade story as a developing cycle of acceptance and rejection of the Witchblade's powers and responsibilities. So first Sara accepts, then uses, then either abuses/or is abused by, then rejects/loses and then accepts the Witchblade again. It all leads to Sara becoming a better bearer. Archetypically, the Witchblade is a Dark Treasure, and there's a lot of potential for framing things within that context. The imagery can still be sexy, but also serve as powerful storytelling imagery.

So here are the first two, which are kind of opposite.

Thumb 1: A literal interpretation of the Witchblade taking a struggling Sara to a place she doesn't want to go. Sara is kneeling in an oily puddle while the Witchblade tugs her into the abyss.

Thumb2: A "level up" picture, where Sara embraces the power of the Witchblade and engages the reader with a kind of "now you're gonna get it" look.

More to come, lemme know if I'm going the wrong way with these.

-Nelson Blake II

-Additional thumbnails
3-Sara and Dani sitting on a rock, but depending on where the story is, I have four takes, all of them with Dani colored in gray tones/monotones, while Sara is in normal color. Cloud type design in the back, autumn leaves in the front
a)Sara in full Witchblade armor/Dani in normal clothes
b)Sara in gauntlet mode/Dani in normal clothes
c)Sara in gauntlet mode/Dani in normal clothes
d)Sara in gauntlet mode/Dani in full armor
4-Same basic idea as 2, with a closer composition
5-Similar to 2 and 4, but with Sara having two Witchblade gauntlets, calling on the idea that she has hers and Dani's to people reading the series, but just a cool pic of Witchblade to those unfamiliar with what's going on in the story.

-Nelson Blake II

One more idea from Nelson - "6-Witchblade tendrils pulling Sara in all directions."

-Filip

right, final cover

Jeffrey Spokes
issue #133 Cover B process

Hey Filip & Philip

Here's a super simple sketch for the idea i'm thinking of doing. It's a fairly straight forward concept of doing really detailed and rendered character studies of Sara as the police officer as well as her in her Witchblade form in the background (she would be colored a bit more faint so that she works into the background while Cop Sara stands out). I'm also thinking of doing some detailed background imagery with patterns derived from the Witchblade weaponry. Anyhow let me know if this works, look forward to hearing your thoughts.
Best!

-Jeffrey Spokes

Hey Filip & Philip

Hope your summer is going well. I'm not sure if you are still interested in getting some art from me, but i was excited about the project and did up a piece. There is still bits of rendering to do on the Armor but i thought i'd send it and see what you thought.
Best,

-Jeffrey Spokes

Hey Filip & Philip

I've got most of the changes done up on the cover, i just wanted to get the green light on the armor that i've sketched up here. I kinda winged the design and wanted to make sure it's what you were looking for.
Best!
Jeff
ps- i'll extend the background so there is more room for the masthead after i complete the armor.

-Jeffrey Spokes

right, final cover

ON THE FOLLOWING PAGES, ENJOY A SAMPLE OF THE ONGOING SERIES
THE DARKNESS®
ON SALE NOW!
ART BY: DALE KEOWN

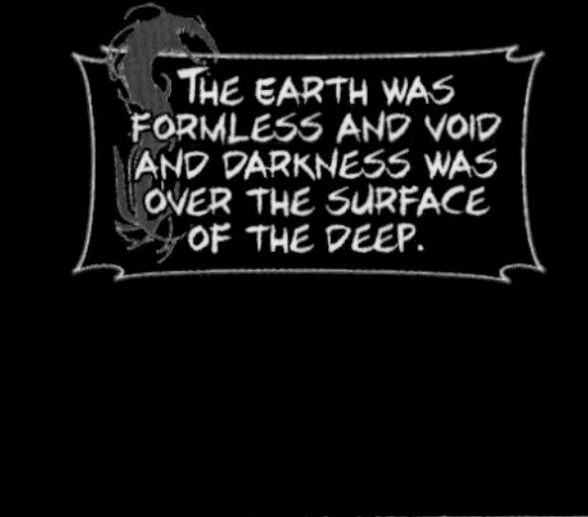

THE EARTH WAS FORMLESS AND VOID AND DARKNESS WAS OVER THE SURFACE OF THE DEEP.

THEN GOD SAID,
T THERE BE LIGHT."

AND THERE WAS LIGHT. AND GOD SAW THAT THE LIGHT WAS GOOD; AND GOD SEPARATED THE LIGHT FROM THE DARKNESS.

AND THE GNAWING ANGER OF THE DARKNESS FOUND NO EXPRESSION FOR AGE UPON AGE, FESTERING, PUTREFYING, DISTILLING TO SEETHING PERFECTION.
UNTIL A VESSEL FOR ITS BOUNDLESS HATE WAS FOUND.
MANKIND.
GOD'S MOST FAVORED CREATION.
THE DARKNESS CLAMBERED
A SCORPION OVER THE
FRAMEWORK OF HISTORY
FOR PURCHASE IN THE
OF MEN, AND FOUND NO
SHORTAGE OF VICTIMS TO

HE DARKNESS SEEPED INTO THE GENES OF A PARTICULARLY ERTILE BLOODLINE AND SLOWLY NCRETED AROUND THEIR HEARTS, FOSSILIZING THEIR SOULS.

EACH NEW GENERATION WAS SET LOOSE WITH NEARLY LIMITLESS POWER AND ONLY ONE CALLING: TO SPILL CHAOS OVER THE WORLD OF LIGHT.

AND WHEN EACH BEARER OF THE DARKNESS CONCEIVED OFFSPRING THE CURSE BOUNDED INTO THE NEWLY FORMED, INNOCENT SOUL, LIKE WOLVES INTO AN UNGUARDED SHEEP MEADOW, LEAVING THEIR OLD HOST TO DIE.

AND EACH TIME IT ENTERED A NEW VESSEL IT STEERED ITS BEARER TO INEVITABLE RUIN.

MURDERERS, THIEVES.

RAPISTS, WARLORDS.

PLUNDERERS WITH LITTLE REGARD FOR THEIR OWN SPECIES.

AND IN OUR TIME IT FOUND HOME IN THE BODY OF JACKIE ESTACADO, AN ORPHAN RAISED BY PIMPS AND KILLERS-- THE FRANCHETTI CRIME FAMILY.
HIS POWERS SERVED HIM WELL IN THE ROLE OF MOB ENFORCER, DEALING DEATH WITH CARELESS GRACE.
BUT AS WITH ALL BEARERS OF THE DARKNESS, TRAGEDY DOGGED HIS EVERY STEP. HE BECAME AN ENEMY OF EVERYTHING HE LOVED.
OF HEAVEN ITSELF.
OF HIS FAMILY.
AND ULTIMATELY OF HIMSELF.
BUT THAT WAS THEN.
THIS IS NOW.

Get the whole story in The Darkness: Accursed volume 1
Available now!

Premium collected editions

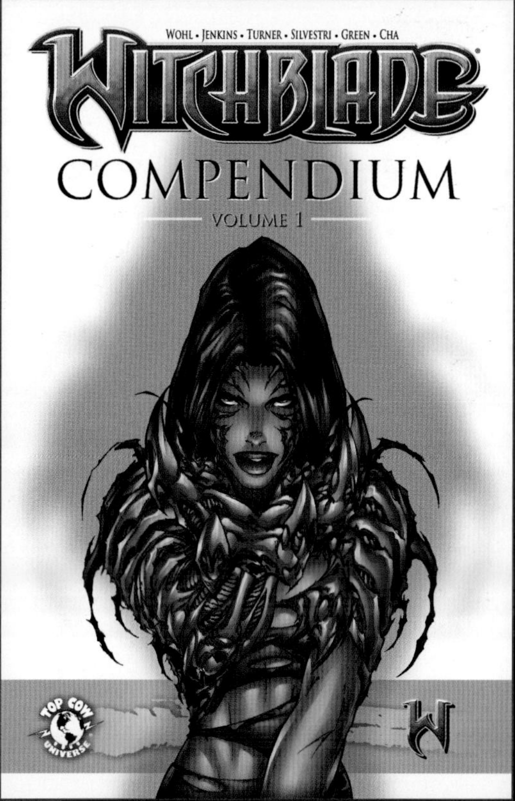

Witchblade

Compendium vol.1

written by:
David Wohl, Christina Z.,
Paul Jenkins
pencils by:
Michael Turner, Randy Green
Keu Cha and more!

From the hit live-action television series to the current Japanese anime, *Witchblade* has been Top Cow's flagship title for over a decade. There's nothing like going back to the beginning and reading it all over again. This massive collection houses issues #1-50 in a single edition for the first time. See how the Witchblade chose Sara and threw her into the chaotic world of the supernatural. Get the first appearances of Sara Pezzini, Ian Nottingham, Kenneth Irons and Jackie Estacado in one handy tome!

SC (ISBN 13: 978-1-58240-634-3) $59.99
HC (ISBN 13: 978-1-58240-798-2) $99.99

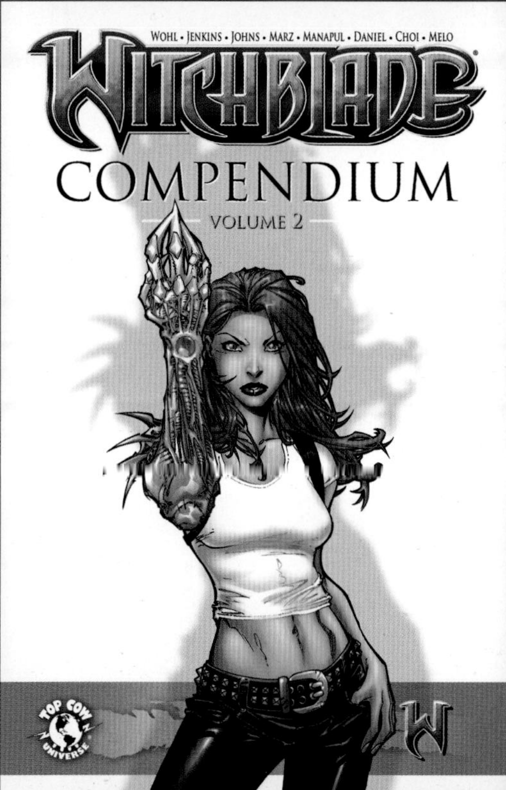

Witchblade

Compendium vol.2

written by:
David Wohl, Christina Z.,
Paul Jenkins and Ron Marz
pencils by:
Michael Turner, Randy Green
Keu Cha, Mike Choi and more!

From the "Death Pool" story arc featuring the death of a major Witchblade character to heading up the NYPD's Special Cases Unit, Witchblade bearer Sara Pezzini and her new partner Patrick Gleason find themselves with more questions than answers as their investigations lead them from haunted museums, dark alleys and forgotten tunnels beneath New York City. Meanwhile, the enigmatic Curator leaves a trails of clues for Sara, ultimately leading her to the explosive origin of the Witchblade itself!

Collects Witchblade issues #51-100

SC (ISBN 13: 978-1-58240-731-9) $59.99
HC (ISBN 13: 978-1-58240-960-3) $99.99

Jump into the Top Cow Universe with The Darkness!

The Darkness

Accursed vol.1

written by:
Phil Hester

pencils by:
Michael Broussard

Mafia hitman Jackie Estacado was both blessed and cursed on his 21st birthday when he became the bearer of The Darkness, an elemental force that allows those who wield it access to an otherwordly dimension and control over the demons who dwell there. Forces for good in the world rise up to face Jackie and the evil his gift represents, but there is one small problem. In this story...they are the bad guys.

Now's your chance to read "Empire," the first storyline by the new creative team of **Phil Hester** (*Firebreather, Green Arrow*) and **Michael Broussard** (*Unholy Union*) that marked the shocking return of *The Darkness* to the Top Cow Universe!

Book Market Edtion
(ISBN 13: 978-1-58240-958-0) $9.99

The Darkness

Accursed vol.2

written by: Phil Hester

pencils by: Jorge Lucas, Michael Broussard, Joe Benitez, Dale Keown and more!

Collects *The Darkness* volume 3 #7-10 and the double-sized *The Darkness* #75 (issue #11 before the Legacy Numbering took effect), plus a cover gallery and behind-the-scenes extras!

(ISBN 13: 978-1-58240-044-4) $9.99

The Darkness

Accursed vol.3

written by: Phil Hester

pencils by: Michael Broussard, Jorge Lucas, Nelson Blake II and Michael Avon Oeming.

Collects issues #76-79 plus the stand alone Tales of The Darkness story entitled "Lodbrok's Hand." Features art by regular series artist Michael Broussard (*Unholy Union, Artifacts*), Nelson Blake II (*Magdalena, Broken Trinity: Witchblade*), Jorge Lucas (*Broken Trinity: Aftermath, Wolverine*), and Michael Avon Oeming (*Mice Templar, Powers*).

(ISBN 13: 978-1-58240-100-7) $12.99

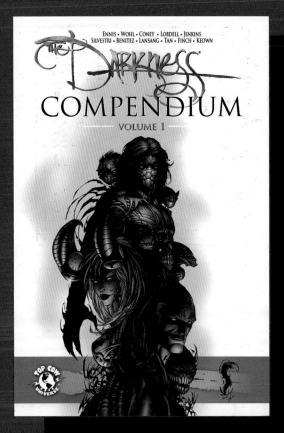

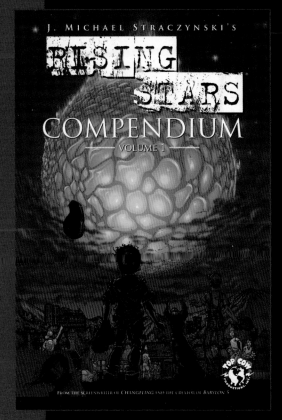

Check out our new "Art of" collections now available from Top Cow!

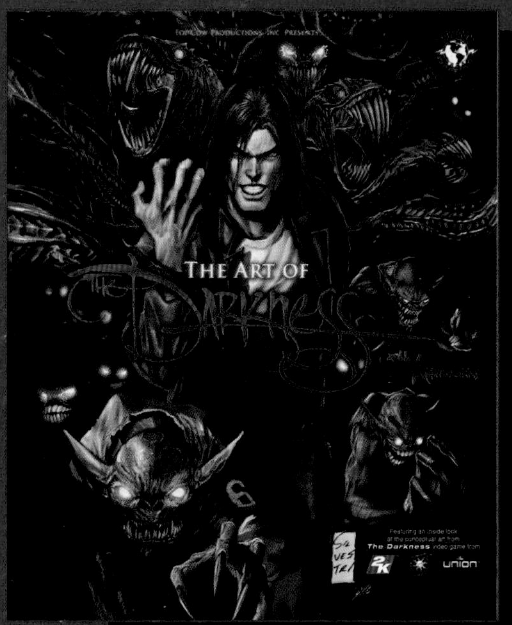

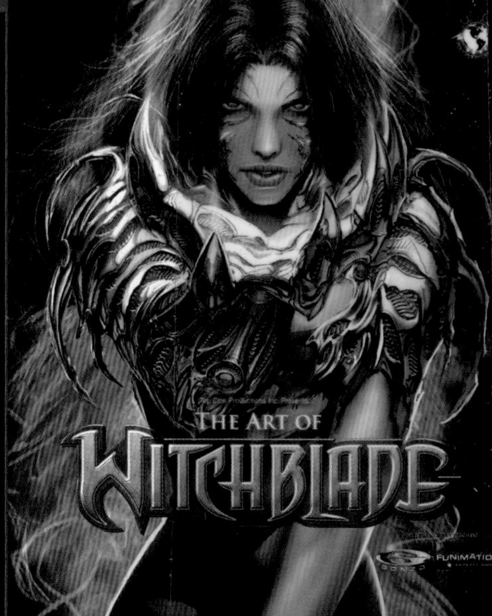

The Art of The Darkness

The Art of Witchblade

Celebrate the ongoing saga of *The Darkness* and *Witchblade* with these deluxe edition art collectior Inspired by "Art of" books for video games and films, these over-sized art books feature glorious illustratio and commentary from the original creators, all contained in a glossy, thick-papered, beautifully designed bo Covers, splash pages, collectible cards, sketches--the very best art from *The Darkness and Witchblade* collect in one place! See it here in its unadulterated form. A decade of work to choose from, these are the definitive "A of" books for *The Darkness and Witchblade*! Featuring art by the top names in comics including:

Marc Silvestri, Michael Turner, Dale Keown, Jae Lee, Stjepan Sejic, Dave Finch, Whilce Portacio and many more!

The Art of The Darkness, (ISBN 13: 978-1-58240-649-7) $14.99

The Art of Witchblade, (ISBN 13: 978-1-58240-857-6) $19.99

The Art of Marc Silvestri

From his humble beginnings as penciler on Marvel' *Conan*, Marc Silvestri understood what it meant t produce a quality comic book. Driven by his commitmen to excellence, Silvestri gained a huge following i the late 1980s on such titles as *Uncanny X-Men* an *Wolverine*. His popularity continued to grow whe he founded Top Cow Productions and had breakou successes with *Cyberforce* and *The Darkness*. Unde his guidance, Top Cow has grown from comic books into a company with ongoing development of vide games, anime and feature films.

Silvestri's decades spanning career has taught him not only the importance of producing quality work, but also the need to foster the next generation of artist by maintaining one of the few working art studi environments in the industry.

Softcover (ISBN 13: 978-1-58240-903-0) $19.99

Hardcover (ISBN 13: 978-1-58240-904-7) $29.99